the 30-second commute:
a non-fiction comedy about writing and working from home

Stephanie Dickison

ECW Press

Published by ECW Press, 2120 Queen Street East, Suite 200,
Toronto, Ontario, Canada M4E 1E2 / 416.694.3348 / info@ecwpress.com

LIBRARY AND ARCHIVES CANADA CATALOGUING IN PUBLICATION

Dickison, Stephanie
The 30-second commute : a non-fiction comedy about writing
and working from home / Stephanie Dickison.

ISBN-13: 978-1-55022-837-3
ISBN-10: 1-55022-837-4

1. Dickison, Stephanie. 2. Authors — Biography. 3. Freelance
journalism. I. Title. II. Title: Thirty second commute.

PN153.D52 2009   808'.02023   C2008-902419-2

The publication of *The 30-Second Commute* has been generously supported
by the Canada Council for the Arts, which last year invested $20.1 million in
writing and publishing throughout Canada, by the Ontario Arts Council, by
the Government of Ontario through Ontario Book Publishing Tax Credit,
by the OMDC Book Fund, an initiative of the Ontario Media Development
Corporation, and by the Government of Canada through the Book Publishing
Industry Development Program (BPIDP).

 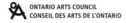

Editor: Jennifer Hale
Cover Design: David Gee
Text Design and Typesetting: Melissa Kaita
Printer: Transcontinental   1   2   3   4   5

PRINTED AND BOUND IN CANADA

ECW PRESS
ecwpress.com

	Name	Artist	Page
1	☑ don't panic	coldplay	001
2	☑ hollaback girl	gwen stefani	005
3	☑ i'm on it (wikipedia)	sudden death	007
4	☑ like spinning plates	radiohead	012
5	☑ work it	missy elliot	016
6	☑ i go to work	kool moe dee	025
7	☑ the taste of ink	the used	029
8	☑ working for the weekend	loverboy	032
9	☑ road to nowhere	talking heads	035
10	☑ subject to change	sum 41	037
11	☑ say it right	nelly furtado	043
12	☑ my neck, my back	khia	045
13	☑ welcome to the jungle	guns n' roses	048
14	☑ cold sweat	james brown	053
15	☑ paid tha cost to be da boss	snoop dogg	055
16	☑ lost in the supermarket	the clash	058
17	☑ big girls don't cry	fergie	065
18	☑ the vagina song	the bloodhound gang	076
19	☑ one thing leads to another	the fixx	079
20	☑ lifestyles of the rich and famous	good charlotte	082
21	☑ all these things that i've done	the killers	085
22	☑ this is how we do it	montell jordan	089
23	☑ wrapped up in books	belle & sebastian	093
24	☑ tongue like a battering ram	faction	095
25	☑ catch me while I'm sleeping	pink	102
26	☑ i woke up with this song in my head...	bright eyes	105
27	☑ please don't stop the music	rihanna	109
28	☑ daft punk is playing at my house	lcd soundsystem	114
29	☑ by myself	linkin park	116
30	☑ mr. telephone man	new edition	118

30-second commute
soundtrack

This is a work of non-fiction.

That said, I have an imperfect memory (the '90s are a complete blur — I may have been Courtney Love at one point), so dates may be incorrect, but generally, it happened around the time I said it did.

As well, to keep the book under 10,000 pages, I've sometimes condensed times and events.

And names may have been changed to protect myself or the guy who ate too much at the restaurant. I assure you I'm not getting all James Frey/Jayson Blair/Stephen Glass on your ass. I'm just telling you like it is — as much as I can on a liter of wine and a pound of foie gras every other night.

— Stephanie

For **Mom and Dad, Ripper and Bogie** — The best family a girl could ask for. Thank you for introducing me to books, art, and culture, and letting me rock out. Somehow I managed to make a career out of it.

And to **Scott Albert** — Thank you for talking to me at a party. And changing everything. You rock my world.

"There isn't a writer who gets an editor to consider his work or, better yet, a real live publishing contract from a press, who doesn't fantasize that his work might take the world by storm."

— *The Forest for the Trees*

don't panic

IT'S 8:35 A.M. on a Wednesday and I am traveling West on the subway. I actually had to push my way on, cramming the already crammed folks into the berth of the train. The first stop is being announced when a baby in a stroller starts making that insistent half cry that says, "Pay attention to me! *Now!*" This continues for all seven stops that I am traveling, along with the sighs and grumbles of the crowd.

I see people stare at the infant with such fury: *This is the only part of the day in which I get to read/sleep/finish my report/do sudoku/have a little quiet to get lost in. I'm beggin' ya, kid, please, gimme a little respite from this crazy world.*

There is a huge gap in the middle of the car. A bunch of us try to make our way over, but we are stopped by people who appear immobilized. What's the holdup, bub? As I shuffle my way into the center as much as the crowd will allow, I am hit by a wave of nausea so violent that I buckle a little. There's a homeless man passed out across a three-seat bench beside the door and people have clearly gotten as close as they can without passing out. There is a wide clearance of a couple of feet.

A couple stands in the middle of the car chest-to-chest, but doesn't make eye contact. It's clear that something's happened overnight or over coffee this morning that has wedged itself uncomfortably between them. The guy reads the subway ads for herpes and tax deductions for low-flow toilets while the girl shoots ice picks his way, daring him to try to explain, or impatiently waiting for an apology that will never materialize.

I am now wedged against the doorway, where a man's sharp briefcase digs into the back of my leg. I try to shift away, but instead sway myself into a large woman beside me. I can't move. The subway jolts to a stop, and the briefcase hits my leg again and snags my pantyhose. I feel the nylon open and run down my leg like mercury falling.

Then a student who is struggling to stay awake, probably exhausted after a night of studying, or working at his part-time job and then studying, drops off to sleep and slumps against my back. I haven't had this much body contact since dancing at the Joker in 1992.

I look up at the ceiling, because I can't stand the breath of the guy facing me. It's like he had raw meat for breakfast. He also keeps smiling at me when our eyes meet (where else am I going to look but straight in front of me). Gross. I consider kneeing him in the balls, but really, there is no room to do anything.

I get off at my destination and walk to my appointment, thinking — *never again.*

Three years ago, I left an office admin job to live out the dream of writing full time.

I had been writing for a decade in the evenings and weekends, and had already been published in many publications and some books, when I decided it was time to make the leap, take the bull by the horns, take the plunge, lay the first stone, make a start, get serious, swing into action, apply myself, jump in with both feet, choose my fate and put my hand to the plow.

Or, in layman's terms, sit my ass in the chair for ten hours a day and write as much as time allowed.

It doesn't sound as exotic or romantic as you'd think, huh?

Yeah. It's *not*.

But when you leave your job, it is the most romantic gesture you can make, like when you decide to move in with the love of your life despite his collection of street signs or beer steins. You are trusting that you can do it. You don't know how, just that you will.

And having the mortgage due every month, wanting to eat good food and buy new discs from Aesop Rock, Blue October, and any number of the Marley offspring helps with that motivation.

But this book is not really for writers. While I am sure they will cling to the few words of wisdom I have about the writing life and look for ways to do anything but what's required (sit down, stare at the screen, and try to make words come out), it is for all of those folks who wonder what a writer's day looks like. After all, that is the question which I am asked most — "What do you do every day?" or "What's it like to be a writer?"

I think it's funny that there is such interest in a writer's life, when most people claim to have a book written in their head, but just don't *have the time to put it all down.*

That's the difference between us and them — we sit down every day and pound out every inch of ourselves while they think about how relaxing it would be just to sit down and write. *It's so easy!* they say. They have *no idea*. They moan about how much they'd like to work at home but what they really want is to be closer to the fridge and television, and not be accountable to anyone. In fact, working at home takes a lot more discipline than you might imagine. You can't let the idea that the sun is shining and there's a strip of stores and coffee shops just a few blocks away keep you from writing the 4,000-word article that's due tomorrow.

I wrote this book because I wanted to reveal all that there is to the writing life. After all, most of the time it's pretty comical. The romantic notion most people have about writing is close in that yes, we are following our dreams and spending days agonizing over words and ideas, but most of the time, we're just barely getting through and often end up writing about increasing the longevity of car tires and how to reduce fridge mold — instead of working on the ten pages of screenplay that we have written, which we believe Don Cheadle would be perfect for, by the way.

Here in these pages, I've written a lot of personal stories — both about the "secret" life of a freelancer, and about my family and friends. For me, writing about my life is much easier than making it up, and I just hope that it is interesting to those other than my parents, who read every book review I write and tell their friends about every article that I publish. I've tried to dispel the myths that you have about us writers and while my life is certainly not that of all other writers, the commonalities among freelancers should ring true. I have had my hand in many writing areas, so the book looks at some of the main ones I've covered — food, music, books, and blogs. When I read similar memoirs, I always long for photos that pull back the veil of writers' lives, desks, and interest in books, but it never happens, so I have included photos of myself and my life.

Sure, I work longer hours than most nine-to-fivers and though I miss having weekends off, I do enjoy the freedom of having a life full of creativity and doing something that matters to me. In the end, it is most definitely worth it. So I continue to try to push my own limits and set goals for more work at the arrival of each new year, but truthfully, I'm a sucker for an evening out with friends at a new restaurant, or sitting on the couch with my fella playing Scrabble.

I'll never make it with this attitude.

hollaback girl

I WHISPER LOUDLY to my fiancé, Scott, "Doesn't she look *exactly* like Gwen Stefani?" He gives me that look. That look that says that the *whole subway car* has heard me. I whisper loudly back, "Who doesn't want to look like Gwen Stefani?"

My insatiable curiosity has always gotten me into trouble, whether it's my long stares at a woman that has managed to somehow pull off sparkly robin's egg–blue eye shadow or asking people I have just met about their morning routine. I spend a lot of time imagining what people do, how they act, how they pick out their clothes. It's odd, I know, but I think most writers spend a lot of time in their heads thinking about other people's quirks, whereas most people spend their time concentrating on their own.

Right now, across from me, a slightly paunchy man in his forties is carrying a host of pamphlets, one of which includes "God, Sex, and the Meaning of Life." He is eating sour cream and onion potato chips from a crumpled bag that he holds close to his chest. The banana-yellow Super Fitness gym bag from the '80s is probably his actual gym bag. The towel emerging from it is a dark sea-foam green, the kind you get at the dollar store on the cheap.

This is the kind of thing that consumes me. Does he live alone in a masking tape–colored apartment where he leaves the television on all the time? Does he have a tired cat that has long got used to all the noise, despite barely a word being passed between the two?

If you think I'm a stalker, don't worry. I'm anything but. I just love to take in rich details quickly, rolling over in my mind what these outer clues could mean about the person within. It isn't just strangers on the subway either. Watching TV on DVD can have serious repercussions for me. After watching the first season of *The Sopranos* in little under a week, I would think about Tony and Carmela like friends I hadn't seen in a while, like, "What are they up to this weekend? Will they get stuck with Artie's same specials at Vesuvio's?" Clearly this is dangerous territory for someone who gets completely wrapped up in details.

I like to think that this is what makes me a good writer — I am curious about human nature and I try to dissect what's being presented to me. That and I want to know everything about everything. And *finally*, after all of these years of absorbing seemingly useless knowledge from reading thousands of books, magazines, websites, and blogs, I am able to use all of those facts in my work. I can write about celebrity relationships (remember Julia Roberts and Kiefer Sutherland?), obscure star beginnings (Brad Pitt on *Growing Pains*, George Clooney on *The Facts of Life*, etc.), and finally dispel myths that people have bought into (Grey Goose promotes themselves as the number-one vodka, thereby eventually securing their place as the number-one vodka).

There aren't many jobs where you can capitalize on your interests, but luckily my passion for books, music, popular culture, food, restaurants, and innovative products has paid off.

As the train enters the station where I am getting off, I wonder what the guy with the gym bag will have for dinner, and whether he and the Gwen Stefani chick will hook up.

i'm on it (wikipedia)

"Wikipedia is the best thing ever. Anyone in the world can write anything they want about any subject. So you know you are getting the best possible information."

— Michael Scott, *The Office*

WIKIPEDIA IS a type-A beast who wants everything just so — coffee cup at a 90-degree angle to the stapler, book edges perfectly aligned, shirt collars stiffly starched. Despite many entries coming from unreliable sources, Wikipedia insists on many strict rules and regulations for making a reasonable entry, which is virtually impossible (much like IMDB, where it took Frankie Muniz or Macaulay Culkin or some once-young thing years to get his photo changed from pimply-faced boy to smug sometimes-working actor).

That's why I have taken it upon myself to write my own entry — uncensored, unabashed . . . and somewhat untrue. But mostly true.

Stephanie Dickison

From Stephapedia, the free encyclopedia

Stephanie Dickison (born October 10, 1971) is a Canadian writer, journalist, essayist, and author. Dickison contributes regularly to many publications and websites, including *The Writer*, *Film International Journal*, PCWorld.ca, and the *Dine.TO* website, where she is a restaurant reviewer and food columnist and has taken over doing Chef Profiles from established critic Sara Waxman. She is co-editor of pan magazine, an online food magazine, and has just published her first book, *The 30-Second Commute: A Non-fiction Comedy about Writing and Working from Home*. She has written and published hundreds of articles, interviews, essays, columns, profiles, features, and reviews for international magazines and newspapers.

According to a 2009 *Random Books for Random People* review of Dickison's book, reviewer Kermit Mulligan wrote, "Her writing is funny and gracious and her timing impeccable. I am reminded of the comedic styles of such greats as Steve Martin and Woody Allen, where melancholy and highbrow humor collide."

With her fiancé, television writer, producer, and all-around sexy hunk, Scott Albert, and lumpy ball of feline love Cosmo all in one tiny apartment, she manages to write, work, and get paid. A little.

Contents
1 Biography
2 Awards
3 Published works
    3.1 Nonfiction
4 References
5 External links

Biography

Dickison was born in Toronto, Ontario, Canada and studied food history and creative writing at George Brown College. Much of Dickison's writing draws from her observations of human behavior, her pop culture interests (hence her PopCultureVulture moniker), her enthusiasm for green living, and, of course, food. Her focus on writing about interesting subjects in an informal and conversational tone has led to a legion of fans and followers of her work. In fact, her work is cited in the Wikipedia entry for rock band Linkin Park, where a quote from her article appears. Her work as a book critic, music critic, and food critic has spanned a decade, yet still people don't know her or seek her out. This might be because she is soft-spoken, blonde, Canadian, or all three.

Dickison was a music critic and associate books editor at the zeitgeist site PopMatters.com back when there were only a few pop culture sites in existence, and has written for publications such as *Paste, Pages, Quarterly Review of Film & Video, Quill & Quire, alive, Tidings, Canadian Literature,* and the *Washington Asia Press* newspaper.

Dickison has interviewed many celebrities, authors, and singers. She lectures at universities and teaches writing to both individuals and groups around the country. She likes it when students bring donuts to class and when there is a board for her to write her name on. She repays the class by handing out copious photocopies, and stays after class to answer any questions. And she'll tell you at least five places to eat if you ask.

Dickison has contributed to three reference books. She contributed two biography entries for *Compendium of 20th Century Novelists and Novels*, two entries in the *Facts on File Companion to the American Novel*, and her essay, "Nick Hornby on Reading," which originally appeared in *The Writer* (v. 119, no. 6, June, 2006, p. 49), was reprinted in *Contemporary Literary Criticism, vol. 243*. Her own book, *The 30-Second Commute* (2009), was published by ECW Press, a publisher known for its pop-culture titles such as those covering the television series *Buffy the Vampire Slayer, Lost,* and *Heroes* and for its plethora of wrestling books.

Dickison was asked to present a paper on popular culture and music at Inscriptions in the Sand '05 Academic Conference in Turkey and her essay "So Many Books, So Little Time" was accepted into the "Scan" issue of *M/C Journal: A Journal of Media and Culture — Australia* (July 2005). She *almost* made it into *Reading Desperate Housewives: Beyond the White Picket Fence* and didn't even come close to making it into other exciting pop-culture books such as *The End of The Sopranos*, *The Shield* collection, and a diatribe on the much-beloved, yet mostly-forgotten *Melrose Place*.

Dickison is not without her critics. The *Ontario Wine Review*'s "Peter Finch Said It Best" made Dickison an example when citing an article she wrote about environmental Tetra Paks for *Tidings*, a wine magazine. Dickison had written, "For convenience and ease-on-the-pocket, you can't do better than a Tetra wine. And from an environmental perspective, you are making a wise choice when choosing the box over the bottle. So if you want an affordable and convenient wine that tastes good and that can be drunk right now, the Tetra is for you." The article argued that Dickison was wrong, and that the wine in the Tetra Paks are "passable at best." But since then, there has a swelling of praise from the media about Tetras. Now they're up-in-arms about twist-off caps instead of corks . . .

She is one of the few restaurant reviewers (along with and well before Restaurant Girl) to forgo a disguise, something that is still seen as controversial despite it being 2009. She is also known for her reviews that are anything but scathing. In fact, other critics say she is not critical enough. Dickison claims to tell it like it is without "tearing a new one" every time she sits down to write up a restaurant. "Besides," she says, "the food I have both on and off the job is mostly great. I dunno what the fuss is about. Toronto's food is fantastic."

Awards

Shortlisted for the Booker T. Award and winner of the Nobel Prize (awarded by advertising firm Chase, Nobel & Patterson) for Best Travel Blog — *Martinis & Bikinis*.

She is a member of the National Book Critics Circle, TravelWriters.com, Canadian Association of Journalists, Writer's Marketing Association,

Access Copyright, a voting member for Independent Dance Music Awards, Endangered Fish Alliance, Toronto Arts Coalition Council, and Writer's Directory, and cannot afford memberships to most professional associations.

She tested recipes for *The Good Home Cookbook* and is a former Certified Fitness Instructor. She also can cut a rug, make a wicked pot of soup from mere condiments and will always send you a thank-you card for the simplest things.

Published works

See www.stephaniedickison.com for full listing.

References

1. ^ *Random Books for Random People*: "Fresh Wit From Unknown Writer," March 31, 2009

External links

- *The Renegade Writer blog Q & A*: Stephanie Dickison
- http://therenegadewriter.com/2006/05/30/renegade-writer-qa-stephanie-dickison/
- *The New York Review of Books*: Stephanie Dickison
- *Writers Manual*: An Interview with Stephanie Dickison http://www.writersmanual.com/show.php?id=1&uid=240
- *New Yorker* Interview with Stephanie Dickison, 2003
- *Comedy Central* Interview with Stephanie Dickison, 2006
- Retrieved from "http://en.wikipedia.org/wiki/Stephanie_Dickison"

Wikiquote has a collection of quotations related to:
Stephanie Dickison

Categories: All articles with unsourced statements | Articles with unsourced statements since January 2007 | Canadian essayists | Canadian journalists | Canadian authors | Non-Members of The American Academy of Arts and Letters | People from Toronto, Canada | People Who Love Food Too Much | Artistic/creative parents | Famous Blondes | Living people

like spinning plates

IT'S ALMOST THREE full years since I've been at home and everything has changed.

Completely.

When I first left my office job, it was to finish a book I'd been writing and researching for five years. I knew I needed full days to get into it and complete it. When I worked evenings and weekends on it, I would have to reread a lot of it and figure out where I last left off. It happened each time I went back to it and I began to feel stalled, stagnated. The only way to do this was to hunker down day after day and do it, I figured.

Leaving your job for something as precarious as "freelance" work is a tenuous step. People will rally for you, telling you how brave you are and how *they* could never do it. Some will try to talk you out of it, fear enveloping them, and its haze making its way over to you — *How are you going to pay the bills? How are you going to generate enough work? What if you hate working from home?*

And truthfully, the simple answer is, there is no way to know until you jump in and just do it.

You can read all the books in the world, including this one, but no one will be able to tell you how to do it. You'll just know when it's time, and you'll do it because you simply cannot live one more day with not trying. It becomes a life and death matter for you mentally and creatively — you feel you will actually die if you don't leave and write.

The other thing is that you will worry about how to leave, when the best time to leave is, and how to tell your bosses and co-workers. And this may extend into months, like it did for me. But like most things, once you do it, you wish you'd done it so much sooner and not spent all those sleepless nights worrying. There's no way to prevent that.

There are many pros and cons to working at home. Here's a short list:

Pro: You get to know the UPS and FedEx guys.

Con: The UPS and FedEx guys get to know you — "You were up late, weren't you Ms. Dickison?" — as you've rushed to the door in a jumble of tangled hair and black nightie. Or worse, straight outta the shower because they won't stop knocking and just leave the damn package on the doorstep.

Pro: You can work whenever you want.

Con: While your friends are out partying it up at the new club with Ne-Yo, you're at home finishing an article about the healing benefits of green algae.

Pro: If you're lucky, like me, you get to work alongside the love of your life. Well, in the next room, at least.

Con: Like the challenge of keeping things fresh when you live with someone, it can be even harder when you're both exhausted from writing to deadline all week. That, and the spaghetti-stained T-shirt you've been wearing since Tuesday.

Pro: You get to read and research topics that really excite you.

Con: Spending the morning reading People. com and other celeb-hounding mags trying to decipher what *really* happened last night with Brangelina at Nobu is *not* research.

No one will be able to convince you otherwise. You will just have to go through it and then try to help counsel others as I have.

And everyone moves in their own time. Since leaving the office, I have had two friends do it too, and they had talked about one day working for themselves for years. Both of them left when it was right for them, when they physically and mentally couldn't take it anymore.

Just like I did.

The whole thing is so dramatic. Because everything is so unknown, it's not like stepping into a job that you've been doing for years. This is a change in *everything* — working for yourself, probably working from home, not getting a paycheck every two weeks, perhaps even for the next couple of months, and dealing with having the *whole day* to navigate your way through.

I left my job at the end of December 2005. On January 1, 2006, I sat down and began writing the rest of my book. I figured it would take three months to complete, so as of April 1, I'd really focus my energy on freelance work — breaking into new markets, learning how to build a website and spending time on lengthier magazine work where I could write 2,000–3,000 words instead of my standard 800–1,000.

There are so many things that you can't anticipate when you make the move from office to home, from part-time to full-time. It's like when you move homes — you may have marked your boxes clearly and called the painters to come in early, but until you're in you don't realize that the bedroom door is unusually small, making it impossible to get the bed, desk, and shelves into the room (you think it may have been the door to the shed in the back), that none of the lights have dimmer switches, and that the extra-long and skinny drawer in the kitchen that you thought would be perfect for tin foil or spices is actually completely and utterly useless.

The best thing about being at home is the comfort level — you can drink coffee out of your favorite mug that holds a cup and a half and fits to your hands perfectly. You can eat whatever and whenever you want. You can pee with freedom without having to enter a password into your computer, or remember your stupid key or swipe card. You can sit in a comfortable chair, and if you want to talk to someone, you can go outside or pick up the phone — there are no co-workers to bother you. You can work to your own body's schedule, getting up and starting work at 5 A.M. if that's what works for you. You can eat at your desk, or work on the couch.

And however much work you want to say yes to is up to you.

work it

ONE THING NO ONE tells you is how hard it is to rid yourself of the old habits that come from working in an office, or that you will still follow your old routines.

Before going freelance, I worked in a doctor's office. It took me three to four months to stop thinking about the office and the patients. It took even longer to rid myself of doing things in that weird way that you do in an office like drinking coffee and chewing gum to stay alert, answering the phone with, "Hello, doctor's office," having wet hair most of the day, and wearing clothes that cover everything appropriately.

You don't realize how programmed you have become to work in that environment. The doctors I worked for had fifty-minute sessions, so I had become accustomed to completing most things in forty-five-minute increments. I hadn't worn a watch for the last five years because forty-five-minute periods had become as much a routine for my body as the ability to answer the phone, type up an intake questionnaire, greet a new patient, and make eye contact with my bosses to let them know that everything was rolling along.

It took a long time to rid my system of its routine. That and the patients' names and needs.

I had worked in that office for over eight years and many people had been coming in the same day of the week at the same time for decades. These were people who didn't like change, which meant that thinking of leaving them was particularly hard. I loved the patients. Even the OCD ones who drove me crazy, calling and confirming their appointments over and over, or the ones who lied about calling to cancel their appointment because despite pulling in a seven-figure salary, they refused to pay for a missed appointment. What I loved most about them is that while some of them did things like drugs, cheating on their spouse, or lying about much of their life, I knew them just as the folks in the waiting room. Some of them were wonderful, despite the problems that came unspooled behind closed doors. I missed them and their eccentricities terribly when I first left. They were entertaining and, because I worked all by myself in the office, they were company. How was I going to fare without them?

There was much about office life that I was *not* going to miss. There were the big things, like having to do menial office work that I thought was beneath me such as cleaning out the office fridge. But over the years the little things, upon reflection, became big things too.

Getting ready in the morning was one. I realize that some people get up at 4:15 A.M., have a two-hour commute ahead of them, and somehow manage to dry and style their hair, get completely made up, make and pack a lunch, get the kids off to school, and throw something in the Crock-Pot for dinner. I honestly don't understand how they do it.

And I'm a morning person.

I wasn't always. I grew up with night-owl parents, and I spent all of my teenage years going to bed in the wee hours of the morning and slogging my way through the day. My mom and I would stay up watching whatever was on TV. She'd call up the stairs, "Bobby's on!" and I'd come rushing down. We never missed *Newhart* and all three of us I think at one time or another believed that we were going to open an inn in Vermont. It looked like such fun. And to help keep the dream alive there was a Stephanie on the show.

We started out watching all the prime-time shows — *Cheers, Empty Nest, Dear John, Coach, The Fall Guy, Kate & Allie.* So many private investigators! So many mysteries to solve! *Miami Vice, Hart to Hart, Cagney & Lacey, Moonlighting, The New Mike Hammer, The Rockford Files, Barney Miller,* and *In the Heat of the Night.*

And it didn't end there.

We'd stay up *waaay* late for the late-night rerun lineup of *Magnum P.I.,* followed by *Simon & Simon,* and then, I think, *Riptide,* which had Perry King, Joe Penny, and some other guy as ex-Vietnam vets who now run a private eye business from a boat. Yeah, it was as bad as it sounds. And it got worse. It descended into glazed-over, catatonic watching of shows like *Mr. Belvedere* (oh Lord), and a show that was just a camera view of getting out of a cab and going up and down streets (and elevators!) of Toronto in the wee hours of the morning set to the sounds of bad, bad, bad saxophone wails. I think after that, it went to the vertical colored bars and tone that signaled the end of the broadcast day.

Maybe it was the tea fudge that my mom made that kept us up with all that caffeine: she'd put some strong Tetley in with a ton of icing sugar and some melted butter, form it into a thick layer in an aluminum pie pan and then we'd eat the entire thing. I think it's an original recipe.

My teeth and temples ache at the thought.

It wasn't until I moved out to my first apartment at age twenty and started working for

---

Ruthie's recipe for tea fudge

Make yourself a pot of tea.

In a metal bowl, stir together:

1 tbsp. butter
1 tsp. vanilla
1 tsp. dry instant coffee

Stir in 1 tbsp. hot tea.
Stir over low heat just long enough to dissolve coffee.
Stir in 1 cup icing sugar (approx).

Eat out of bowl with spoon.

(To make fudgier, leave to set for about one hour.)

a publishing company at 8 A.M. that I transformed myself into a morning gal.

I can see the romanticism in staying up late and writing, but for me, that's a slippery slope to not getting things done. But for some writers, it's the only way of life. So now I get up somewhere between six and eight most days, depending on how late I was out the night before, but the 4:15 A.M. thing only happens once or twice a year when I've been able to get lots of sleep and go to bed early.

But back to getting ready for work.

For the office, I would get up, have a shower, and get dressed all in about half an hour, and head out the door. With wet hair. I worked with wet hair for over eight years. And thus, I looked pretty much the same for close to a decade — hair slicked back in a ponytail or bun with black eyeliner (think the Robert Palmer girls from the "Addicted to Love" video). It became a thing where if I dried my hair and wore it down, it was for a special occasion in the evening.

And the same with my contacts. It was so much easier just to slap on my glasses than take the extra time to put in contacts, so I wore my glasses for most of my work life. Again, if there was a special occasion, I'd put them in. Now I dry my hair every morning and wear my contacts about half the week. It is like a whole different world.

Another major difference is eating.

When I was at the office, I had a couple cups of coffee and a toasted bagel in the morning (thank you, Tim Hortons), and a sandwich for lunch. I didn't take a lunch, so I had to eat things that were easy to scarf down using one hand so I could do other things or eat while I walked to the bank, or worked in the backroom pulling files, or checking expiration dates on boxes of antidepressants and anxiety medication.

I gained a lot of weight at the office. Even though I was eating whole wheat, rye, or pumpernickel bread instead of white, two sandwich-y things a day took its toll.

That, and I ate throughout the day. I was out of the office a lot, burning a lot of energy through the stress of working with two demanding doctors, and even more demanding patients, each with their own needs and peculiarities. This routine ate up my energy so much that by the end of a seven- or eight-hour day, I was completely spent.

I didn't bring anything from home, so I depended on being able to pick up something while I was out, so that I always had something at my desk. Hence, the sandwich that was always on the CPU under my desk that I could nibble at when the waiting room was empty or the patients were in session. I'd always panic if I wasn't going to be able to go out and get something. We were on the tenth floor, so it's not like I could just step outside quickly. The doctors wanted me there at all times to see to the patients. It could be hours or even until the end of the day if I didn't plan it right.

One of the most enjoyable aspects of being at home for me is being able to eat whatever I want, whenever I want. I drink only one cup of coffee a day, but drink hot tea all afternoon. I snack throughout the morning, then stop and have lunch with Scott (which is his breakfast because he stays up later and sleeps in later), and then we have dinner together whenever we feel hungry.

I don't panic about having enough to eat throughout the day anymore, and I eat salads, soups, pad Thai, and crunchy vegetables — things that I couldn't really eat at work. I also can wander into the kitchen and graze on whatever suits my mood — nothing like that what's-available-at-the-horrific-food-court dilemma I used to face daily. And though it took close to a year, I lost what Scott referred to (albiet lovingly) as my "office thighs," which had come from walking while eating, and sitting and stressing.

And peeing is a lot better too. Sometimes I'd have to wait for a patient, or someone would need me, or I'd be stuck on the phone. Now . . . I just go.

Of course my favorite bonus about working at home is being able to see Scott and our big cat, Cosmo. Although I sit at my desk from the time I get up til just about dinner time, I appreciate their being around, their company — even if it's in the background. I wasn't sure if all of us being at home at the same time would work out — after all, we live in a one-bedroom apartment — but it's great.

Scott is a freelance television writer. He writes at his desk in the living room, and I work at my desk in the bedroom. And although we work in separate rooms, we can lean back in our office chairs and shout out to one another about something we've just read on the Net, or ask a question about grammar or spelling. It's kind of like *The Office* — Cosmo is Toby, and Scott is Jim, and I of course am Pam. No! Michael. No! Phyllis! Yeah.

I like having my guy around. Most people that we tell our work situation to are stunned into silence, or immediately reply that they could *never* do that. Yeah, I wasn't so sure that it was going to work either, but you don't know until you try, and luckily, I love spending time with Scott, whether it's at "the office" or going out for dinner "after work." There are those few times when we've both got deadlines at the same time, and we're in the apartment for days without going outside that I find I need a walk just to break up the monotony and to stretch my achy legs. But usually it's sheer bliss.

And our cat Cosmo kind of goes between the two of us, either sleeping at the edge of the bed near me, wanting to sit on my lap as I write, or lounging out on the theater chairs near Scott's desk. It is nice having the company of an animal around, and I think every workplace should have a cat or dog nearby to pat and rub every once in a while.

And then there's being able to wear what you like.

Now I'm old-school and cannot work in pajamas, unshowered with no makeup. Writing at my desk all showered and dressed makes me feel professional and ready to work. When I get to my desk in the morning, I am ready for the world in proper attire (and that's a good thing, because the UPS and FedEx guys get here pretty early), but I realize that for most people, dressing for work is not enjoyable.

I can understand that, but unless you work in a very corporate environment, even tellers at the bank these days dress in incredibly casual clothes. It all started to go downhill when "business casual" came in. We went from the actual definition of the term — suit and shirt, no tie — to khakis and blue button-downs, to jeans on Fridays, to pants with rips and sneakers, and miniskirts, and sometimes even flip-flops.

Nuh uh.

But I realize it can be hard to navigate today's requirements for dress, especially when it's getting more casual all the time. Who (other than myself) wants to be the most dressed-up person in the room? And so, most days while I'm not in a full suit at my desk, I am ready to head out the door at a moment's notice, which turns out to be necessary many days.

In *Glamour*'s January 2007 issue, for "What will you wear to work today?" Marisha Pessl, author of the great book *Special Topics in Calamity Physics* said, "Contrary to popular belief, not all writers dress like retired librarians. Whoever said that you can't be serious, smart, creative *and* incredibly fashionable?"

I agree. However, all that sitting takes quite a toll on your clothes. In the book, *Mockingbird: A Portrait of Harper Lee*, author Charles J. Shields wrote that Nelle (Harper Lee) "claimed that the effort to write the book had worn out three pairs of dungarees."

There are other differences in the home office. The supplies here aren't always as luxurious as having your own supply cabinet or having a limitless budget from which to work. But while you have to buy your own calendar and schlep off to Staples for your own supplies, you do have the advantage of having things that you like, things that are pretty and actually work.

At the doctor's office, I had a sliding keyboard tray that never slid. It would pop out and I'd have to finagle the little clamp fixtures underneath every time I wanted to slide it back under my desk (read: every time I had to leave my desk for something). It was a small thing, but it annoyed the hell out of me. It was just one of many things like that, that you have to put up with in an office environment.

While I love having my own filing system, laptop that I picked out, and all the materials and non-essentials that I want, I don't have a company expense card that someone else is paying off. This means I try to buy all of my supplies when they're on sale and keep spending to a minimum. Whoever said being a writer requires just paper and pen is lying. Sure, that's all you need . . . unless you actually want to be a *paid* writer.

The aggravation of working in Microsoft Word spans both worlds, I'm afraid. I type in "ringtones" and it suggests "ring bones." I type "Belinda Stronach," and it asks me if I want to change it to "Stomach." The Canadian spelling for "cheque" makes Word and Paper Clip really mad. *Did you mean "cherub"?* I dunno. Would American Express accept a "cherub" for $43.86? Word, however, knows how to spell Scorsese and Schwarzenegger. Scary.

Now here's something that you don't think about working from home — the noise and interruptions that occur.

I'm sure that if you've done any dreaming at all about working from home, it includes quiet and serenity, and time to think. Perhaps your scenario even includes candles and Michael Bolton playing in the background. But when you spend the whole day at home, your workspace morphs into a a cacophony of noises and interruptions totally different than an outside office.

For one thing, the hot water in our building often gets turned off during the day to facilitate repairs, so the super will knock to say that there will not be any water for the next hour or two. Now normally I have been up and showered before this happens, but it does infringe on washing my hands, making a cuppa tea, or, ahem, peeing.

It doesn't even occur to people that this could be going on because it doesn't affect them. Today I met my neighbor Allana at her work for lunch and told her I'd got the hot water knock. She had no idea that occurred during the day, unless they'd planned on it and sent a memo ahead of time. But the knock comes and the hot water goes, Allana. Oh yes it does.

The other hard part is either repairs going on in the building or outside on the street. We live on a major street that is often having its hydro poles removed and replaced, cement sidewalk cut up and repaved, and the area near the curb dug up to put in more Ethernet cables, or whatever they do down there. And of course if the repairs are in the building, sometimes it's just easier to leave and work at the café down the street or the library. I have fantastic noise-canceling headphones that I sometimes wear to insulate myself, but sometimes even they are not enough to compete against the jackhammers, drills, and buzz saws. (Sure, your office building may experience the sounds of the city too, but I bet your walls are thicker and your windows don't open.)

I haven't even mentioned the deliveries and phone calls that occur throughout the day.

Who knew that working at home could end up being like *Extreme Makeover: Home Edition*?

So while I may have stopped answering the phone like I did at the doctor's office, I still have a long way to go to figuring out how to be a good boss to myself and work at home amid the cement drilling, sirens, and general chaos of downtown living. These things can happen in a regular office too, but at home I can pat Cosmo, listen to him purr, and feel the stress melt away.

i go to work

"Things are okay when the things you complain about are the things you used to dream about."
— TV screenwriter Aaron Sorkin recalls an acquaintance's remarks

WORKING AT HOME should be easy. The coffee pot's right there. You don't have annoying co-workers hovering over your desk soliciting relationship advice. You can work when you want without having to be a slave to the clock. But there are battles for sure.

As soon as I wake up, before I even open my eyes, I am thinking about writing — either projects that I am working on, or something new that I can't wait to get onto the page. This doesn't mean that I float to my little desk, begin typing perfect first drafts and complete award-winning assignments each day. I kick and scream my way through page after page, thought after thought. But my motto remains the same as another blonde coot, Helen Gurley Brown — "Get up and do it if it needs to be done, even if you hate it!"

And then it's time for lunch.

every site that i went to in one day (or what i like to call "complete disclosure")

ecwpress.com
google.ca
youtube.com
tpl.toronto.on.ca
powells.com
thedistrict.ca
gottheknack.blogspot.com
blogger.com
hallmark.com
mac.com
hipstercards.com
amazon.com
annickgoutal.com
portolano.com
yahoo.com
toneka.com
ecinewyork.com
hellomagazine.ca
signaturevacations.com
rogersmagazines.com
variety.com
sephora.com
people.com
timeinc.net
flickr.com
nymag.com
peeledsnacks.com
answers.yahoo.com
about.com
nytimes.com
nutrition.about.com
cbc.ca
us.penguingroup.com
instyle.com
npr.org
bbc.co.uk
guardian.co.uk
highbeam.com
theage.com.au
flyporter.com
wireimage.com
imdb.com
dine.to
sagawards.org
hbo.com
cbsnews.com
accesshollywood.com

It is incredibly hard to come up with original ways to describe a band that's already received a ton of press or translate the way a note sounds onto the page. Interviewing a celebrity who responds to questions with gruff one-word answers and trying to wring a thousand-word article out of mere *yes*es and *no*s is excruciating. But some of the time, not very often, it is that kind of feeling that stand-up comics talk about when they've "got the room" and their set ends with a crushing roar of applause and adulation. That's what I chase after with each and every piece.

That and the $200 that will pay for this week's groceries.

There is no book that tells you what to expect in setting up your writing life — where to focus your time and energy, and how to plan so that you are always working on what will move you ahead, what will interest you. There are tons of books about freelancing, and some are fantastic, but there is no way to know what your days, weeks, and months are like until you take the leap and try it on for yourself.

The couple of my friends who've done it this past year both say how busy it is, how all-consuming and exhausting it is. And I think if you really want to be successful and make a living at it, that's true. It all depends on what kind of writing you're doing and what else you have going on in your life.

If you have kids, you've got to work around their schedule, which results in probably less time overall to get the work done, but while the kids are out, I'll bet your time will be used more effectively than mine. My friend John is a crime novelist. He has written three well-received books in the last three years — all written at home while his boys were in school for those couple of hours in the morning and then a couple of hours after lunch.

I need some kind of system like that . . . though giving birth and then raising two boys seems a little excessive.

Maybe working at an outside office would help. I'd have to get it all done while I was there, making my time spent way more effectively.

Part of the problem with working at home is the number of temptations for procrastination. At an office, you are working for someone else. And while you might not mind your work, you probably dream of having your own inn or flower shop, or of rebuilding old cars instead of doing what you're doing to pay the bills now. And there's that innate office thing — as soon as your boss closes their door, you pick up the phone to talk to a friend, or go online and start pricing luggage.

At home, you can flop out on the couch and watch television if you want to. Ways in which writers procrastinate have become legendary and the source of many jokes. But while I do goof off occasionally, I rarely procrastinate, for one very good reason: I am my own boss right now. If I don't work, I don't get paid. I, and not someone else, am in charge of the work I do. And if I don't do it, there are a ton of writers out there champing at the bit, so I don't really slack off.

But I do get distracted online, just like everyone else. While I don't surf aimlessly, I do get obsessed by certain things and spend time looking them up (it's not my fault I know every TV actress who has played the girlfriend or best friend in every TV sitcom — Paula Marshall, Nikki Cox, and Carla Gugino, I'm talkin' 'bout you). I

have a firm stance on not doing Facebook and surfing the Net —
wasting time on People.com and the like. Really, I watch only the
very occasional music video on YouTube.

And then I get back to work. There will be no flopping on the
couch in front of the television for me!

Although, have you seen the last season of *The Wire*? Holy
#@%!

the taste of ink

EVERYONE THINKS that they can be a writer. And everyone wants my job.

Cate Blanchett once said, "Ultimately, people are just interested in your performance. Nobody wants to see your homework." With writing, it is the complete opposite — strangers will come up to you and ask you about craft, process, your muse, everything they can think of because they are hoping, *praying*, for that little nugget of wisdom that will change the way they write and lead magically to their writing "The End" on the screenplay that has been lying beneath their single bed for the last twenty-two years.

I have no quick fixes, miracles in a bottle, or overnight success stories for you. In fact, the rest of this book is mostly recipes for flank steaks and bouillabaisses, a little diatribe on the subtleties of Steve Martin's writing, the total underappreciation for Angelina Jolie's clavicle, and the hotness that is *Friday Night Lights*.

But one thing for certain is the landscape on which writing has been built. It is now greatly written, accessed, and dissected online.

So much is changing — Gen Y (age twenty-six or younger) is blogging about Obama, Hannah Montana, and how to hack the iPhone, while my generation (X, ages twenty-seven to forty-one) continues to try to stay hip with My Chemical Romance messenger bags, piles of books by Chuck Palahniuk, Jonathan Lethem, Chuck Klosterman, Jonathan Franzen, and David Foster Wallace (apparently, Gen X loves its books by guys named Jonathan, or Chuck, or David), and hobbies that include mastering coq au vin, collecting wine, redoing our open-air live/work spaces in streamlined chocolate shelves, and covering every surface with stainless steel. In other words, doing stuff to make us appear cooler than we actually are.

This means that every writer can now carve out his or her own niche, be it copywriting (a hugely lucrative way to go if you want to make good money), screenwriting, or even blogging about Britney, Lindsay, and Paris's tirades (Perez Hilton, TMZ.com, and even *People* magazine have made millions off just these three).

But that doesn't mean the work is going to be good or stand out from the crowd.

There is now a glut of writing — about everything from heavy metal fans in the Netherlands to how to peel squash efficiently. It doesn't have to be interesting to you. But someone out there is circling the font blogs, writing about flora and fauna wallpapers and updates about the latest Archos portable media player. So to be a lifestyle writer — fashion, beauty, technology, travel, food, and pop culture — is a tough area to tread now, because *everyone's* doing it. And there are people who spend all day, every day writing and breathing about cupcakes, Jay-Z's latest projects (how does one person do so much?), and the latest spa destinations. Sure, I spend most of my day writing, but I'm all over the map. I can't be following Jay-Z's every move (though that would sure be fun and *finally* Beyoncé and I would have something in common).

So I've tried to eke out a niche, a style, a way of writing about what I think the crowd wants. And for someone crashing close to her forties, I'd say I'm doing pretty well with my Paramore CD, my chicken-wing USB drive (because why have a regular one when you can have one that looks like a chicken wing?), and my knowledge of everyone currently releasing a hip-hop album or starring on a Disney program (how many tweens with impossibly white teeth can there be?).

My job as a pop culture writer is to write about not only what's happening now, but what is *to come*.

And that's why my office is filled to the brim with new face creams, workout shoes, socks made out of Bubble Wrap, and why I can usually be found at my desk with my headphones on, rocking out to the latest CDs by Sia, Vampire Weekend, Shawty Lo, the Kooks, and, sadly, the Jonas Brothers, the Cheetah Girls, and *High School Musical: The Soundtrack*.

working for
the weekend

TODAY IS ONE of those crazy days where I am just scrambling to get things done.

That writing at home is all about getting ten hours of sleep, eating three healthy, solid meals a day, and letting inspiration cloak you while you write incredibly moving essays is ludicrous. There have been one or two days in my career like that, but it's as rare as an Arsenio Hall sighting. Often I am rushing around, hair flying in different directions, shirttail hanging outta my skirt, just like people working in an office. Just like you. My heart pounds outta my chest on Monday mornings. I fly out of bed, flinging the duvet across Scott and Cosmo, who are sleeping peacefully amid the noise coming out of my chest. How can they just lie there when so much has to be done?

It's weird, isn't it? You'd think I'd be more relaxed because my schedule is my own, but I know what needs to get done in order to keep on track, stay ahead and meet my deadlines. I am after all CEO, owner, PR manager, and full-time employee. And you'd think

See, at least I look busy.

weekends would be better, but unlike most office folk, I'm at my desk working. I have deadlines on Saturdays and Sundays, and if I don't, I'm using the weekend to either catch up or get ahead on something. It's work time, whether it's the weekend or not. However, from having worked in an office all of those years, I still have that Monday-to-Friday mentality so when Friday at 5 P.M. comes, I feel a huge rush of relief. Scott and I usually go for dinner, a walk, or to an event. It is really the one time during the week that I don't feel guilty for not working. The rest of the week I feel bad for simply taking a lunch break.

Some people let the spirit move them or decide to call writing something else, like Heather Sellers, author of many books about writing. In *Page After Page*, she writes:

I treat my writing life like a fabulous, enchanting lover, because that is what it is to me. Something that is terribly time-consuming, delicious, and time-stopping. I have missed important meetings for love, and I will continue to put my writing life in the same position. My writing life is the lover at the center, not the neglected cranky demanding millstone, my ball and chain.

When you are in love, truly and passionately, you don't have to write down in your daily schedule *Spend quality time with Lover today.* You can't not.

And that's the secret to a happy writing life.

Having a writing life is like having a fabulous lover. You find yourself not paying bills on time, not showing up for boring things, spacing out during tedious conversations. Why would you go anywhere else?

I appreciate her ability to be all whimsical, but I can't imagine being able to get anything done this way, all woozy and free-spirited. I have to approach writing like work, otherwise I'd just spend my days in libraries and bars, gazing and dreaming, which, let's face it, is how I spent all of high school.

Playtime is over, Dickison.

road to nowhere

I LOVE conversations in cars.

Something happens when people talk in cars. Someone says something offhandedly, something that otherwise would have gone unsaid. They reveal secrets, tell of frailties and lies. Marriages that you thought were as sturdy as oak are suddenly unveiled to be on the brink of demise.

I believe that these conversations unfold because you often aren't looking at the person to whom you're speaking. You're looking straight ahead at the oncoming road and traffic in a space that's small and intimate. It feels safe to say almost anything.

That's how I feel about writing. It is like I'm behind the wheel, staring straight ahead and anything can happen. My friend, Ava, says that being in the passenger seat and watching things whiz by puts her in a meditative state, which she concurs can make you say things in the car that you wouldn't otherwise. "It's like drinking, and things just come pouring out," she tells me, laughing, eyes all a-twinkle.

When I am writing, I am able to talk about my interests without fear of being made fun of or ridiculed. I can geek out over a new font (have you *seen* Vtks Untitled or WC Sold Out A Bta?), or write about the history of Cobb salad without worrying about what you think. I know it may not mean much to you, but these things excite me. Just like the game *Dungeon Explorer: Warriors of Ancient Arts* for PSP and Jessica Alba flick thrill you. I can write about issues without interruption or having to acquiesce to someone else's opinions. And learn further about things I'm curious about.

And yes, finally I can spend my days waxing poetic about the subtleties of Ryan Gosling's eyebrow acting, Chandra Greer's sumptuous stationery store in Chicago, and Toronto's most enticing pork dumplings.

Somebody's got to do it.

subject to change

LOTS OF WRITERS know from an early age that this is what they want to do. Scott's mom has papers from his primary school where he writes that he wants to become a "writer" in a steadied, tried hand. She has a collection of amazingly well-written, engaging stories of his from that early on.

Both my parents are artists, so I grew up believing that that's what I'd do too. I went to a high school that had a specialized arts program, so instead of shop, I was life-drawing from real nude folks in ninth and tenth grade, and making clay bowls in eleventh grade.

It turns out that after years of drawing and dreaming of becoming an artist, I wasn't actually very good. I could draw something I saw well enough but I had no sense of composition, color, or anything really original. I didn't realize this until about grade 12 though. While all my friends were selecting universities and planning out their lives, I was trying to figure out not only what I was going to do now, but who I was.

I turned to the theater program at school because it was still artistic and there were cute boys. I had also always wanted to be a star and had practiced my Oscar speech a number of times (it didn't bother me that I had never even been featured on someone's answering machine, much less a film). I did a wrenching scene from *The Doll's House*, complete with shaking and tears, but somehow it didn't translate to my classmates, who sat in stunned silence and then went back to talking about the new Benetton rugby shirts. As a result, the medley of scenes that we did as a showcase at the end of the semester had me playing Marilyn Monroe, Vanna White, and "Girl Ironing." I was to say, "Did I leave the iron on?" complete with head tilt — the epitome of dumb blonde mythology.

It bothered me, but not enough to speak up. I was madly in lust with a fellow actor and this meant that we got to be onstage together. It was so raw and exciting. My tight faded jeans complete with large knee rips and oversize teal Le Château sweater trailed back and forth across the stage a lot that season.

I joined a teenage acting troupe and we launched a version of *Fame* where all of the dialogue and songs were ripped straight from the movie. I stood in for the occasional actor but ended up as stage manager and liked being in charge for once.

Only problem was that my boyfriend had broken up with me and was now seeing one of the lead actresses.

Aaaand . . . scene.

Theater didn't hold my attention for long after that for more reasons than the skinny boy — I couldn't remember my lines, I hated costume changes, and the constant flakiness of my fellow actors grated on me like Macy Gray's man-voice. I did do a brief television appearance on a CTV morning show, but my heart knew I didn't have what it takes to do it for a living.

So I graduated from high school and didn't know what to do.

Because this was the '90s, I worked at a cappuccino bar (the early '90s were all about cappuccinos, cigars, martinis, and pesto). I spent a lot of time at the radio station upstairs, relearning how to work the boards for the late and early morning shows and do playlists, etc. After my twelve-hour shift I was spending all of my free time at the station. I was considering making it a full-time thing when the CRTC fired a bunch of people, including the VPS of stations. Yeah, they weren't going to need me anytime soon.

So I started applying for office work. I still wanted to do something artistic, but I didn't know what to do next. I couldn't find anything creative to do that didn't involve heavy breathing into a phone receiver to a desperate man on the other end, so I opted for admin work.

I temped for a short while for a mostly retired geologist who had an office in a beautiful old building downtown that looked like it had at one time been a bank.

Under a layer of thick dust the old, dull-colored office looked like it had remained untouched since the late '60s. There was so little to do there that one day I reorganized the entire office, dusted

somebody told me

You're going to read a lot of advice over your career about how to write. For example:

- write a thousand words a day (four pages). It's only four pages, five days a week. It won't kill you. You can't "fall behind" and you can't "get ahead." Every day is a new thousand words
- do two hours of revision five days a week for the rest of your life
- do three pages of longhand writing, strictly stream-of-consciousness every morning
- map out a year of magazines you want to write for

I've read hundreds of books about writing in my role as a reviewer for *The Writer* magazine, and I can tell you that most of them say the same things over and over. It doesn't matter what *other* people are doing. It's up to you to sit down and write and find out what works for *you*. I have made up my own system and so will you. And while it's helpful to read what others are doing, it doesn't mean that their template will suit you.

So while I wish I could fill up this book with page after page of how to be a writer, all I can say is: read a lot, write a lot, and do things that you love with people that you love.

It all gets put into the mix and somehow you end up with a pretty great recipe.

off a computer that seemed like it had never been turned on, and updated the record-keeping system. The kindly old man was clearly used to how the woman who had worked for him for thirty years did things.

I didn't get called in again.

It didn't even dawn on me to pursue writing when I snagged a job at Doubleday Publishing Group. It's not as glamorous or Jessica Stein–sexy as it sounds. I worked in the "New Member" department.

You know those annoying little cards that fall out of magazines offering five books for ten dollars and then you'll be sent the selection of the month for the rest of your days? I inputted those names, numbers, and addresses into the system. There I was working underneath the then-tiny publishing offices of Doubleday and it never occurred to me to be a writer. I came into the office at 8:15, chatted with the only other person in my department, a wonderful woman named Noor, and left at 4 P.M.

It was pretty awful.

I was there for just over two years. It was the first and only time I ever worked in a big office. The old, battered wooden desks were laid out in rows like a schoolroom and we all faced the front like some weird cult headquarters. I worked almost exclusively with middle-aged women, which introduced me for the first time to:

- Avon catalog shopping for everything from sunscreen and lengthening mascara to sweaters and automatic can openers
- cards passed around and money required for every circumstance imaginable (sure, birthdays I can understand, but we were supporting people's kids and husbands with our daily "donations")
- polyester pants. Everyone wore 'em but me. You heard people before seeing them
- a work cafeteria, which was heaven — hot, homemade food for insanely cheap prices, and tea and coffee for a quarter. Those were the days.
- what middle-aged women did. They had kids to pick up from

school, husbands to care for, parents to worry about, and jobs that they hated. These women didn't eat out at restaurants every night. They made roasts or set their slow cookers before leaving for work. The lovely older woman behind me, Lila, would have the same Swiss Chalet meal (quarter chicken dinner, dark meat, with fries and extra sauce) delivered every Friday night for her to enjoy while watching *Diagnosis Murder.* She wore a lot of lavender.

It's good that I left when I did. I had moved out to my first apartment when I got the double-D job, and had found such joy in cooking for myself and others, and having the space to read and try to search for what I wanted to do.

I launched my own catering business to such success that I had to close. My last gig I'd had the oven on for three days straight and I was hallucinating from the exhaustion, heat, and having to fill one more canapé crust. I took some food history and cooking classes at a nearby college and at the same time enrolled in a creative writing course. I didn't have any notion of what I wanted to do still, but I was thirsty for intellectual and creative stimulation.

I left Doubleday to work for a lawyer in his small, cramped duplex that was lined with piles of discoveries, file cabinets bursting with legal-sized documents, and everywhere Styrofoam coffee cups still half-full of coffee. It was chaotic in there, but a welcome change from the purple-turtlenecked world of Doubleday. And the money was better. The days were long, but I lunched on homemade cabbage rolls, stuffed peppers, and moussaka from the neighboring Greek restaurants and went back to my one-bedroom apartment feeling like I was at least moving ahead financially. One day I was working away and had apparently transcribed something incorrectly. The lawyer screamed at the top of his lungs and threw a full telephone book at me.

I left right then and thought how much I'd miss the homemade Greek food of the area.

That and a steady job.

Eventually through my parent's fantastic neighbor, Marlene, I found work at an organization called Parents for Youth: Helping and Supporting Parents (PFY). Marlene is a group leader for parents with out-of-control teens and also is a psychotherapist. She recommended me when the position became available. This was 1992, I think. And I worked there on and off just until a couple of years ago, and still pick up voice mail when longtime employee (and my best friend) Victoria, is away.

It was here that I learned how helpful counseling can be. PFY groups were held at the offices of a psychiatrist and his psychotherapist wife, who both saw patients with severe trauma. The things I saw and heard were absolutely horrific, but what I got out of it was how these lovely folks were able to help those who so desperately needed it.

I was hooked. The work was administrative but interesting because of the patients, and I was able to work on my own while still having contact with people every hour or so. I met my best friend Victoria, for whom I am so grateful, and got an extended family with all those who worked in the office over the years.

From there I went to work full-time at the doctor's office described previously — a hypnotherapist and psychiatrist — for eight years. I knew that doing patient intakes and answering the phones wasn't something I was going to do for the rest of my life, but I was seriously worried that I wouldn't do anything that really was "me." I took more cooking and writing classes and spent a lot of time reading and researching my interests at the library. I never figured it would amount to a career, but I knew nothing would ever happen if I didn't take the initiative first.

So I did.

say it right

WRITING NON-FICTION doesn't seem as romantic a notion as writing fiction or poetry, I know, but in real life Wesley Snipes is still running from back taxes (is that where the "running man" comes from?), someone actually created a device called the Coneivore (a tool to use to pick up pinecones in the backyard), and there are socialites in New York actually named Binky Urban and Celerie Kemble Curry.

The one good thing about the world done gone crazy is I don't have to make any of this stuff up (which is good, seeing as I'm exclusively a non-fiction writer). Plus no one would believe me if I did. It's good to be a non-fiction writer in today's pop culture–driven world. Why would I want to do anything else?

Except that recently, non-fiction's biggest prize went to an account of life in Baghdad. Apparently my writing about Rick Mercer, Hollywood Tape, and Greening Your Bathroom just ain't gonna cut it. And using ain't and gonna for comedic effect isn't helping either. Sigh. Chuck Klosterman, Amy Krouse Rosenthal, and I will not be

Just an average day downtown.

at those fancy book galas. We'll be at home watching *Family Guy, The New Adventures of the Old Christine*, and *The Office*.

But I like that I can change subjects with my mood and indulge in my interests. Also, in just a matter of an hour, I saw a man with an actual feather in his cap, a person carrying a naked mannequin torso, and a guy looking very seriously at porn videos and magazines at 11:22 A.M. on a Tuesday morning.

And because of the nature of my work, I can go home and write it all down. And get paid for it. I think I'm gonna write me a non-fiction comedy.

So much for my shot at the Samuel Johnson Prize for Non-fiction, Charles Taylor Literary Prize in Non-fiction, National Book Award, Kiriyama Pacific Rim Book Prize, Pulitzer Prize for Non-fiction, Governor-General's Award for Non-fiction, Grub Street Book Prize in Non-Fiction, *The Guardian* First Book Award, National Book Critics Circle Award, Whitbread Book Award, *Los Angeles Times* Book Prize, and *Boston Globe-Horn* Book Award.

my neck, my back

(with apologies to my parents and in-laws)

"Sex is one of the most wholesome, beautiful, and natural experiences money can buy."

— Steve Martin

ONE OF THE areas that I don't get to write enough about is sex.

Not in a technical fashion of course, but in that pithy, funny manner that those twenty/thirtysomething women who live in New York, or the columnists for *Esquire*, *GQ*, and *Details* write.

There's such a plethora of material, but not a lot of markets outside of hardcore stuff that looks scary or like it hurts, or the mainstream stuff like *Playboy* that seems to favor mostly well-known writers or celebrities.

So, up until now, I hadn't had much of a chance to exercise my funny sex muscle.

That sounds weird, I know, but you know what I mean.

But where else can you find so many euphemisms for the same thing — and so many of them that are soooo bad? They can be divided into two categories I find — the oldies and the goodies.

The oldies include: parking the pink Cadillac; inserting tab A into tab B; dancing the married man's cotillion; filling up the gas tank; exchanging DNA; gettin' yer freak on; docking the rocket in the space station; the twist and shout; organ grinding; doing arts and crafts (yeah, I don't get that one either).

And the goodies or more recent additions to the vernacular: docking the thumb drive in the USB; occupying Vagistan; and putting a snake on her plane.

I know.

Ugh.

But still funny, right?

And then I thought, Well, those spam e-mails I get are so badly written. Maybe there's something in that. I mean, I can do better than this:

From: reflus

Subject: Greeting writerscramp

I have been successfully helping men like you to enlarge their penises since 2000.

Although Reflus (I'm assuming it's like the Swedish version of Rufus) has been doing it for so long — eight years now — that perhaps it's a legit business venture.

Or this one:

From: hima Rives

cc: Kawilarang Damocles

Be a supermacho! Charge your one-eyed monster for 110% and have a lifetime fiesta with Ur girl!

I have to admit, even I wouldn't have come up with 110%. That's good stuff.

Maybe it's harder than I thought. I mean, there are so many ways to go. There's long and super descriptive, like this one:

Subject: Get life-like better than real pussy masturbator!

It so hard to find a virgin nowadays. With the Personal Puss! your dreams come true! Ordering your Personal Puss! you'll receive a virgin pussy and experience new sensations of breaking the hymen.

Enjoy lifelike sensations with a specially designed to feel like a real pussy hand held masturbator. The Personal Pussy can be fucked any day and any time. Made of best modern materials it is reported by some men to be better than the real pussy.

Or there's the kind that get right to the point like this one: *Order the best fuck thing ever.*

Until I figure out how to work this into my freelance writing career as a sex columnist or sassy television host, I'll continue to love and learn from my sex spam.

I mean, how can you beat this?

Subject: love general magic stick

Your little soldier will grow up to a big love general!

Turn your trouser mouse into a one-eyed giant with this brand new medicine.

You will work wonders in bed with your new long and stiff magic love stick.

She will love a massive meat in her back door!

Sigh. I've got some homework to do.

welcome to the jungle

WRITER'S DISTRACTIONS are unique to the individual. Some people will go for a walk, watch TV, clean the bathroom and mop the floors, or simply lie down and read until they "feel" like writing. I don't do many of the above, though I will rock out at my desk with headphones, go to the library, shop for food with my mom, or look out the window throughout the day, watching the taxidermist across the street. That taxidermist has come to represent for me some of my worst fears, but also the immense change that can be brought about by a writer's words.

When I first moved into the building five years ago, I was terrified of all things stuffed and I would look at the shop across the street with immense and immobilizing fear. This was a fear that had been manifesting itself for much longer though. It had started as a kid.

My dad was a newspaper editorial cartoonist, but in his "spare time," he illustrated book and 'zine covers for science fiction, fantasy, and horror authors, and so I had images of monsters, ghouls, vampires, and the like as part of my childhood mental landscape and surroundings. This didn't bother me so much, but somehow it didn't desensitize me to scary things either. I was a terribly sensitive kid and ran screaming out of the movie theater during a screening of *Benji*. Apparently they were merely *threatening* to kill him and that was enough for me.

Actually, all Disney movies became impossible to watch — the witch in *Snow White*, Cruella de Vil in *One Hundred and One Dalmatians*, and the sad life of Dumbo had me weeping in theater lobbies, bathrooms, and out on the sidewalk in front. My poor folks. They were just trying to be good parents and take me to a show.

On top of this, I was afraid of anything that was animated, or looked like it could be animated. My parents took me to McDonald's and Mickey Mouse came out to greet all the kids. Somehow I knew it wasn't the cartoon come to life, and figured someone was lurking inside, but who? Scared isn't a big enough word.

As I got older, it affected where I could go. In grade school, we had a school trip to Niagara Falls, which also involved a visit to the wax museum and the haunted house. Well, statues were a huge problem for me: if they looked at all lifelike or real, I was worried about them coming alive — a big theme in horror writing — and so the whole haunted factor was a definite no-no.

Despite my pleadings to stay on the bus, the teacher made me go. I got about two feet inside the door and by the time I became enveloped in the dark, someone screamed and jumped out, and I was off. Hysterically crying, running blindly down darkened halls through cobwebs with arms reaching out, I was suddenly grabbed by one of the adult chaperones, who took me out a side exit. I spent the rest of the time in the souvenir shop, buying rock candy and the biggest pencil I'd ever seen (I still had it up until five years ago — they NEVER run out, but sharpening them is a bitch). There, I really had a nice time. Until I came across the stuffed tiger made out of real tiger fur . . .

For a couple of my early teen years, my parents and I would go to a sci-fi/horror convention where my dad sold artwork and people like Peter Straub, Don Grant, and Charles L. Grant (no relation) would speak on panels. We stayed in a university residence in Rhode Island,

and other than people often dressed in costume and Frankenstein makeup, it was a lot of fun. They had all-you-can-drink Mountain Dew with *crushed* ice and an arcade that never closed.

It was an eleven-year-old's dream.

In 1982, they screened *Halloween*, or some other now cult horror flick, and I remember being scared just being on the same floor, worried that someone would open the door and I would somehow see the slashings, maimings, killings, and bloodshed. (I can't be more specific because I still haven't seen it. And won't. *Ever.*) So I played arcade games by myself while the adults watched the movie. Centipede is a lot of fun, but wrist fatigue sets in quickly having to scroll that big yellow ball all over the place, even if you're just a wee little thing. So I hit the pool tables to knock the balls around a little. My dad plays pool like a pro, so getting in a little practice time was not time wasted. A wickedly tall man with thick glasses and just-got-out-of-bed hair walked up to me and asked if he could play too. Sure, I shrugged, in that aloof kid manner that seems to last well into teenhood and then come back sharply in your sixties.

We hacked the balls around and were just finishing up the game as the door to the theater room opened and people came pouring out, talking excitedly about the film, gesturing wildly, making hacking/slashing motions.

Shudder. Glad I'm playing pool with the weird guy, I thought.

Like Paul Newman in The Color of Money.

That weird guy was Stephen King.

Later that day, he was seated at a small desk, signing books for a line of fans that rivaled those at Disneyland. He politely signed books, but obviously was painfully shy. I know this because I was too. He came to the convention a number of years after that and I knew that he was ultra famous, but to me he'd always be the guy whose ass I kicked at pool. (I'm sure he let me win, the big lug.)

The man responsible for half the books lining bookstore shelves.

As a woman in my thirties, I remain easily scared by the littlest things and every once in a while I try to be really brave and face my fears, but I don't usually get very far.

There was an Internet thing where you watched a supposed film trailer for a thriller, and then your computer would act up and all of a sudden a scary guy came out at you from the screen. I survived only because I watched it during the day and Scott and Cosmo were nearby for consoling. If I was alone and it was dark, a heavy, maybe even illegal prescription drug would have had to have been administered. And yes, I still screamed when he jumped out, but I'm okay.

And I can be in a room with a bearskin rug or life-size statue now.

(Hey, it's small, but progress nonetheless.) Taxidermy used to have the same effect on me — I'd see a stuffed moose head on a wall, and my arms and legs would get all numb, my vision would blur, and I wouldn't be able to move out of sheer fear.

But Susan Orlean changed all of that for me.

A fantastic writer for the *New Yorker* and author of *The Orchid Thief* and *The Bullfighter Checks Her Makeup* (to name just a few of many), she wrote a wonderful essay about going to a taxidermy convention. I was scared to even read it, but this was one of those small steps toward facing my fears, like going in the ocean at night in the Dominican Republic, eating fish eyes, and watching documentaries about genocide and other inhumanities.

She spoke about the people behind the grizzly bears, deer, and geese and how many of them actually care deeply for the animals that they work with — that this is their way of preserving their beauty. It doesn't sound very convincing coming from me, but Orlean makes it happen on the page like no one else. And reading her words, I realized the power a writer can have.

And so now, I can watch the taxidermist across the street work on his animals and I don't feel like fainting. He works late into the night, which, of course, made it so much creepier. But now I think about Orlean's words, and I find myself leaning against the painted window frame with a small smile sneaking its way onto my face. I see the swan that he's been working on for months and am enamored. It is truly beautiful. At least all the way up here on the third floor.

And when someone delivered a black box to his door yesterday afternoon, those old fears remained in the closet with my old diaries, jeans that I can no longer fit into, and former boyfriend's love letters. I saw only hope in the black box. I don't know what was in it, but I can now see how it will be transformed into something beautiful.

But don't expect anything stuffed and/or preserved up on my wall anytime. I've come a long way, but I'm not there yet.

I mean, have you *seen* Slipknot?

Ack.

cold sweat

"I think I did pretty well, considering I started out with nothing but a bunch of blank paper."

— Steve Martin

THIS IS ONE of those rare times that occurs about twice a year.

It's where so much work piles up that for about three days, I feel completely overwhelmed and immobilized by what's ahead. I do some easy work, believing that it will get me thinking in new and strategic ways again. I stay up late reading, reasoning that reading someone's brilliant work will somehow rub off on me. It usually takes three days for me to work out the kink and to feel that I'm back to my normal self again.

It's hard, but I try to be patient with myself. After all, I've seen this all before and know that I will somehow make it through.

That's the weirdest thing about deadlines. If I get too many at once, or a particularly large one is looming ahead, I panic — wondering how I will get it all done. I make lists, drink a lot of coffee, and silently pray for a way to find the road to completion. And somehow it all gets done, despite the thoughts bouncing around in my head — *There is no way I can do this. This is too much for one person.*

This is why people in their thirties have heart attacks. Maybe I should have a shot of whiskey for strength and courage. *It'll be fine. You get it done each and every time. You're putting too much pressure on yourself. Relax, Dickison[1]. Have a glass a wine and take the pressure off. It will happen if you just let it.*

To tell you the truth, there is no one thing that I do. There is no single answer. Just put your head down and do the work. Do badly until the good comes. Sometimes the not-so-good gets published along the way, and you have to just let that be, otherwise you'd drive yourself crazy (and you'd never get anything in print).

And after the work is done, for a moment let yourself relax and enjoy the feeling of accomplishment — or at least the feeling of being done. You deserve it. And besides, first thing tomorrow morning, you're going to have to get right back to it.

Maybe pour that drink after all.

You're going to need it.

---

[1] You may have noticed that I refer to myself by last name only a lot. I was in the Air Cadets from age twelve-and-a-half to nineteen. With a ratio of boys to girls 75:1, I learned to take orders and toughen up pretty fast. I also learned that I can do anything boys can do. Better. While wearing lipstick and a pretty dress.

paid tha cost
to be da boss

"To make a film every year is not such a big deal. It doesn't take that long to write a script. I write every day. I'm very disciplined. I enjoy it . . . I have a perfectly sedate life. I wake up, do my treadmill, have breakfast, then I write and practice the clarinet and take a walk and come back and write again and turn on the basketball game or go out with friends. I do it seven days a week. I could never be productive if I didn't have a very regular life."

— Woody Allen, quoted in *The Forest for the Trees*

I LEARNED MORE about writing during one year of doing it full-time than the decade that I spent writing afternoons, evenings, and weekends while working.

And quite honestly, I've learned a great deal about myself.

When I quit my job and lost all the security I had to write full-time, I had no idea what to expect, or even whether I could do it. And now I know it's what I'm meant to do. I first left the shackles of working in an office full-time at the end of December 2005, while I was working on another book. I finished it, then edited it all, and for the first four months of 2006, that's all I did. I had a few magazine articles and columns that had been previously assigned, but otherwise, I just focused on the book.

After April, I queried my heart out and wrote every day, really focusing on getting into new publications and working with new editors. I got some really exciting assignments but made very little money. Scott was supporting me with the money he was making from television scripts, so I just focused on getting as much new work as I could, and didn't worry about what they paid.

It is hard being your own boss, and I am harder on myself than anyone else. I don't allow excuses or mistakes. I push myself pretty hard. But there comes a point when you just have to be good to yourself and take each day with humility and grace. And there's one thing that is often hard to remember when you are your own boss: writing is supposed to be *fun*.

This is something that I talk about with other writers often. We work so hard chasing that next job that we sometimes forget that our time is ours to do what we want with it. And, despite our complaining, we get to spend the day writing, creating, and thinking — exactly what we always wanted to do.

I have those days where I manage to balance it all and feel like I accomplished a lot both in writing and with life stuff, but it's not often. I struggle to worry more and do more and then worry less and let more go. I don't have an answer on how to do it well, only that I wake up each morning striving to make *this* that perfect day. And although I manage to see friends and go out every once in a while, I'm usually at home writing. It's a tough slog a lot of days, but mostly it's blissful in a hard-work-is-its-own-reward kind of way.

Writing at home full-time is not for everyone though. Ned Vizzini, author of *It's Kind of A Funny Story*, had a full-time job, wrote in the evenings, and loved it. He then quit his job and took on writing full-time. It was so hard on him that it landed him "in the nuthouse."

Despite the constant flux, I will continue to cobble together freelance work and write every day. That, and I will try to slow down every once in a while so I can enjoy my accomplishments instead of just focusing on the next job. I need to feel my life changing bit by bit instead of just blowing past it working to deadline.

That ain't no way to live. Just look at what it did to Spalding Gray, Ernest Hemingway, and Sylvia Plath.

lost in the supermarket

THERE ARE A LOT of things to consider about your schedule when you work at home.

Making meals at home is healthier, but you have to buy and prepare all that food, so there is a whole new time factor that you have to consider. You may have all day to write now, but a big chunk of that day will be spent prepping, eating, and cleaning after two or three meals a day. Suddenly grabbing an prepackaged sandwich is sounding pretty sweet, eh?

And because you have the whole day, it is easy to fill it up with everything other than writing. There are bills to be paid, laundry to be done, and groceries to pick up.

I decided that as a freelance writer, with the whole day mine to fashion how I desired, I could create the perfect day. I began the following morning with paying bills, throwing a load of laundry in, and cleaning before getting down to work. I figured if I got it out of the way, then I'd have the rest of the day to really focus on the work. I made Scott and me a terrifically healthy lunch and two hours later,

This is what my office looks like. A pile of:

- file folders
- brochures
- press kits
- business cards
- menus
- catalogs
- letters of all kinds — my parents, friends, and some business correspondence
- PR postcards
- invitations
- lined paper pads filled with notes and ideas
- Post-it notes with illegible reminders of things that had to be done long ago
- photocopies of recipes and articles
- pretty journals with only the first three pages filled in
- library books with pages marked to go back to and make notes on
- magazines — you wouldn't believe how many magazines
- applications for professional association memberships, grants, and listings on various websites
- newspaper articles that I want to expand upon
- printouts of e-mails that I need to copy down information from
- bank statements
- bills of varying amounts
- manila envelopes filled with copies of magazines that I've contributed to
- masses of sheets of Call for Papers for academic journals and books
- printouts of song lyrics (for singing along while I'm working. I'm still a teenager at heart)
- sheets of stamps
- envelopes
- rough drafts of articles I'm working on
- research notes for my book and articles I'm working on
- hand-drawn maps of restaurants, PR events, and meetings
- notices of visual and performing arts events
- journalism conference information
- agendas for upcoming trips, conferences, and media events
- pamphlets for discounts of business cards, letterhead, and combined yoga/ Pilates classes that I plan to attend but have yet to go to
- encyclopedias
- reference books and periodicals
- cue cards with notes from recent talks I've given
- writing workshop outlines
- manuscripts of friends' books
- review books
- diary that I vow to start any day now

I got ready to go out. I did a big grocery shop and went to the post office mid-afternoon, thinking that it would be less busy, so it'd take less time.

I got home at 5 P.M., unloaded the groceries, and then started prepping dinner. Two hours later, I was finally cooking, called Scott, and told him when it would be ready. We sat down for an hour and then there was the supper cleanup. By 8 or 9 P.M., the last thing I felt like doing was writing.

So that all had to change pretty quickly. Many writers I know struggle with being in charge of their own schedule. For me it's a constant battle as every day is completely different, which doesn't help matters.

My time is divided between writing for magazines, pitching to magazines, updating my food and personal websites, and managing my daily blog where I review new and fun products and services. Added to that is a little editing, reading books for review, reviewing restaurants and conducting chef and celebrity interviews, and attending press and industry talks and events.

And let's not forget all the phone calls, e-mails, writing up invoices for finished pieces, and correspondence. Oh, and then there's home stuff — cooking, cleaning, grocery shopping — and spending time with Scott, family, and friends. It can all be a little overwhelming.

The tricky part is finding time to actually *write*.

When I worked at an office, I would never have dreamed of bringing work home, but now I work all the time, both because I love what I do, and because it's right there. At the end of the bed, no less. A couple of months ago, Scott and I were writing for so long during the day, every day, that we had to instill a mandate that we take Sundays off before we lost our minds. We did it once . . . and then couldn't find the time to do it again.

If I don't have meetings though, I can easily sit scrunched over my little desk for twelve hours, which is not at all sane or healthy.

I have a little something called "I'll just do one more thing," and it's been pretty hard to shake. If I don't have a meeting or a restaurant to review, then I'm likely to stay affixed to my desk, except to take a break to play with Cosmo or fix something quick to eat.

It's the same if I have deadlines. I stay glued to my desk, head down, and you wouldn't believe how quickly time passes when you're clacking away at the keyboard with deadlines looming. It makes me start to miss the days at the office, where the hours would *crawl* by and I couldn't wait to get home. I know there are writers that use timers to sit and work for an hour at a time. My problem is that I wouldn't hear it. Four hours later, I'd look up and wonder why I felt so hungry, or why my shoulders ached.

At first, having the whole day free to do what I wanted was exciting, especially after having been bound to my desk working on the book for four months straight. I went to the library when it opened at 10 A.M. and shopped for groceries in the early afternoon before the crowds. I met with people over lunch, and was out at various times during the day. It was wonderful. Scott was often working on scripts at night so I'd write until eleven or so, and then go to bed at 11:30 or midnight. I was still writing eight to ten hours a day but over an extended period of time.

Soon though, I was feeling the pressures of writing after dinner. Often, after having been out for much of the day, I didn't have the energy of the early morning, so I was struggling to complete pieces. I felt all turned around. So after working much of the year like that, in the fall I changed my workday back to working at my desk for the bulk of the day and then going out in the evening to run errands, etc., with the rest of the world.

That worked for a few months and then the restaurant reviewing I was doing really picked up. I was heading out to restaurants three, four, and sometimes five nights a week. In addition, I was starting to go to a lot of media events for various publications, which took up the rest of my nights. Meetings got shifted to late afternoon and occasionally over lunch. All of a sudden, most of my day was spent away from home.

That presented a whole new challenge. How can you write for eight to ten hours a day when you are out for that amount of time?

It's even harder now. I am out at meetings and in restaurants

Cosmo helps me with my filing.

anywhere from twenty to thirty hours a week. And I have more writing work now than ever. Plus a book to write in just a matter of months.

Eep.

Perhaps I sound like your retired parents/grandparents, complaining that I have too little time despite having the whole day, each and every day. But I am not the only one struggling. I met with my friend who writes a travel column for a major newspaper, who just left her full-time job at a law firm a few months ago. Already she is struggling to find enough time to complete all of her work. She has two young kids so she has far less time than I do, but we each have our unique challenges to overcome.

I am coaching a woman in a different country who writes full-time. She wrote a book first, and is now trying to write articles for magazines and newspapers. Like my friend and me, she too is trying to find enough time to write.

It is a constant struggle that plagues writers. Each day is completely different and though I may set out to work on five certain things, circumstances can change and all of a sudden, I am out for the bulk of the day, yet the deadlines remain the same.

Weekends are difficult to navigate because on the one hand, it is a fantastic time to get work done and catch up on the things I couldn't do during the week. But then there's the fun factor. I mean even if you're working, you can feel the weekend in the air — people are sleeping in, brunching, shopping. There's no avoiding the weekend vibe.

There is a condition that causes someone with a brain injury to be unable to see anything on the left of them (or the right). It's called left neglect (or right neglect) and sometimes I think I have regular life neglect when it comes to work. I forget that there are people at home, with their feet up, watching *Dancing with the Stars*, eating Cheetos, and thinking about what kind of cargo pants to get at the mall.

The optimum way to work, I think, is to block your time into different sections so that you're working an hour on one thing, three hours on another. It enables you to focus your energy on the work in front of you without feeling that you should really be doing something else (I multitasked for years before realizing you don't get more done after all), and it allows you to work on more than one project during the day.

The hard part is sticking to it. I am so often on the go that I can get caught up in running around and forget about the importance of planning ahead and following it. One lesson I learned early on is do not use a scheduling system that's not natural for you. It's tough enough to do everything that needs to be done without writing stuff in the wrong day or spending hours trying to learn a new calendar system. Also, change your system as often as your scheduling requires it. My first year at home I bought four different systems because I didn't know what I needed until I found it.

Anytime I'm about to complain to myself about looming deadlines or how difficult it is to write, I just have to think of Jean-Dominique Bauby, who used to be the editor for *Elle France*. He's no longer the editor because he had a massive stroke in 1995, was in a coma for twenty days, and was paralyzed except for one eye, which he used to write the entire book *The Diving Bell and the Butterfly* (later made into a movie) by transcribing it with a series of blinks (he died in 1997).

That and Angelina Jolie's book, *Notes from My Travels: Visits with Refugees in Africa, Cambodia, Pakistan, and Ecuador*. It's enough to make me want to call up the Humane Society and just start giving my time to legless puppies and blind Dalmatians and avail myself to any humanitarian association that will take me.

That's why it's important to get away from concentrating and writing all day. You can start to lose your focus, and lose touch with reality.

The work gets done somehow, but maybe you should block in a little time for YOURSELF.[2] And I'm going to follow my own advice. This weekend we're getting together with friends, tomorrow night Scott and I are going out for dinner, and on Sunday I'm planning on doing *nothing*.

Yep, I'm pretty excited.

I'm taking care of me. *Finally.*

I'll just do one more thing first . . .

---

[2] I know it sounds like advice for high-powered stockbrokers or real-estate agents, but this goes for us creative folks too. Just because we're writing doesn't mean we shouldn't take it as seriously as other professions.

big girls don't cry

"Finish every day and be done with it. You
Have done what you could. Some blunders
And absurdities no doubt have crept in;
Forget them as soon as you can. Tomorrow is
A new day; begin it well and serenely and
With too high a spirit to be cumbered with
Your old nonsense. This day is all that is
Good and fair. It is too dear, with its hopes
And invitations, to waste a moment on
Yesterdays."

— Ralph Waldo Emerson

THE DIFFICULT DAYS of a writer are a punch in the gut, a toe
stubbed a thousand times, and a head bang on the corner cupboard
that results in blood.

I don't want to get too dramatic, but the life of a writer itself is
tough enough without editors telling you how badly you suck, how

unoriginal you are, or that you didn't make it into yet another magazine. Most days are not like this, but there are some that may well knock the wind right out of you.

I got my first restaurant reviewing gig with a prestigious magazine and I'd had to work hard and long to get in there. A lovely woman hired me and gave me the rundown — I could bring someone, order two appetizers, two mains, two desserts, and a half-liter of the house wine.

Because the work is done anonymously, I had to try to "discreetly" take the menu and keep the notes in my head. If I had to write anything down, I had to make it look like I was doing something else. There were instructions on making the reservation (no real names), tipping, and paying the bill. I took it all very seriously, and was incredibly nervous and excited. I was now a "professional," and was ready to show 'em my stuff.

I was lucky enough to have been assigned a swanky Toronto restaurant in Yorkville, and Scott got to come with me. I was absolutely thrilled to be going somewhere together we hadn't been. I was slipping into a little black dress when an e-mail came though from a guy, saying he was the new editor, blah, blah, new policies, changing everything, blah blah.

I panicked. Should I still go? What should I do? I e-mailed him back, figured that I'd go, and the worst that would happen was that they'd pay me and not run it.

We went and had an okay time, though we were tentative about everything.

I went home and over the next two weeks wrote my ass off. With only seventy-five words and certain of areas that I was required to cover, I didn't have much room to be creative or much leeway to fuck up.

The magazine paid me and didn't run it.

It was bad, but I pulled myself up and kept on applying for food writing work. I knew that I knew food and no one could take that away from me.

And sure enough, a few months later, I landed a gig with someone else reviewing restaurants and started being the go-to food gal for a couple of magazines.

I knew I could do it. Eventually.

I once had to write biographical entries for a reference book. I selected romance authors because I thought that they were probably just like all writers, and it was a complete change from the mainstream authors I was already familiar with. But have you seen how much they write and under all those different names?

I chose two mid-level writers, which was hard work enough, but then I chose one of the most popular authors, Nora Roberts, because I thought that at least I'd be able to find information on her. Just trying to put her books in chronological order was a complete nightmare — there were book title changes depending upon the publisher, whether it was paperback or hardcover, and what country the book was published in. This was all in addition to her numerous noms de plume. It was like trying to gather information on a secret agent.

It took me months of long, dreary nights of dredging up information, making sure it was correct, putting it into chronological order (which was made even more difficult by not being able to just sort it under the name "Nora Roberts" — where does *this* one go?). I then had to synopsize each of the 100-something titles, which as you can imagine, all being in the romance genre, all sounded suspiciously like the same book.

Now this is by no means a diss to Ms. Roberts. In fact, I am incredibly impressed by the amount of work that she puts forth. It is amazing to me that someone can write that much and have multiple books come out a year. You might be thinking that's because it's romance and it's not difficult to write. Oh yeah? Let's see you throw down 300 pages in three months and see how easy it is.

After about three months of continuous work, I sent it to the editor, eyes brimming with tears from exhaustion and sheer frustration. It is seriously one of the hardest things I've ever had to do. Two weeks later, I get a long e-mail detailing all the changes that had to be made. The formatting was not the only thing wrong, apparently.

Oh, did I mention that the original formatting was *completely different* than what they were now asking for? Yeah, this happens a lot. Try to not punch your computer screen. If you must, scream into a pillow or go for walk. It's not going to change the fact that you have to sit down and do it. Again. It'll just allow you the space and time to go back to it.

Over the next few months, the back and forth went on and on, and of course it was from a different person than the original editor who had now left (eyes brimming from frustration, I'm sure), so this new person and I had no history/chemistry/interpersonal connection. It was basically like having to start from scratch.

Breathe. Deep breaths.

So I opened up the document — again. I could barely stand to look at the screen, as seventy-five percent of it now had to be changed. I managed to make it through (and I'm proud to say that no alcohol was used, though I did go through jars of pickles and bags of baby carrots — crunching my way through the madness), but it was tough.

There are worse things — the situation in Darfur, yellow nail polish, fur coats worn with running shoes, Heather Graham's wide-eyed-Jennifer-Aniston-hand-flapping acting — but I was still left empty and exhausted. It didn't get published and I was never paid for it either.

Fuuuuuuck.

Once, a piece that I wrote for a *Desperate Housewives* collection didn't make it in, but it wasn't because they didn't like it.

I had spent months e-mailing and writing them about the project, and after completing what I thought was a funny and observant piece, I constantly checked online to see when it would be released. I received the generic e-mail sent out to all of the contributors as to when to watch out for the book. They didn't have any questions about the piece, so I assumed they didn't do a lot of editing. Fine by me!

Months went by and I'd still occasionally check to see if it was available to order. After all, being a pop-culture writer, this would be the credibility I needed to get me from unknown writer and critic to perhaps getting a column in a magazine, or at least an assignment from one. When I finally saw the completed published book on Amazon.com (it was an academic book, so it's not like I could just whip down to my local bookstore to get it) my heart punched through my chest and up into my throat: my name wasn't on the list of contributing writers.

I e-mailed the editors to ask why and they replied back with a huge apology letter that explained that they had never received it and if there was ever a second edition, I would be included.

I felt a little better that they liked the piece and *would have* published it. However, after that nanosecond went by, I fell right back to being depressed about it. The fact that I didn't end up in the collection, no matter what the reason, didn't further my career any and my status as "Pop Culture Vulture" continued to go unnoticed and uncelebrated.

Technology is great when it works, but when it doesn't, it makes me want to pick up a sledgehammer. Or a really stiff drink.

But then the anger dissipates and I go back to texting on my smartphone, while ripping music on my laptop and writing the latest installation of my fitness column.

I continue to love my electronics despite their occasional failings.

The editors had changed over the years, and well, eventually someone probably just got sick of seeing my name land on their desk, so they said yes.

It only took me eight years, but I got in.

I handed in the assignment on time and awaited a response.

I received an e-mail that said:

Hi Stephanie,
Thanks for your interest in writing reviews for our magazine. We've currently got more reviewers than available assignments, but I'll definitely keep you in mind for future reviewing opportunities.

Just FYI — we pay a flat fee of $125 per review (300 words). We're currently on deadline for our Sept/Oct issue, but I'll see if I can get you into our Nov/Dec lineup. If you want to check back with me in a few weeks, I should know more then.
All best,

I e-mailed her back and received this:

Hi Stephanie,
When assigning book reviews for the magazine, I sometimes take title suggestions from reviewers. Do you have any Nov/Dec titles you'd especially like to review? Let me know.

I spent a number of hours poring over *Publishers Weekly* and going through book websites to come up with a bunch of titles. I sent them off, completely spent.

I got this as a reply:

Hi Stephanie,
Thanks for the title suggestions. I've actually got a ton of non-fiction already lined up. Do you have any fiction titles to recommend?
Best,

Hmmm. Let me just come up with some suitable titles off the top of my head without doing any research. That should be easy. Just one sec. This time it took twice as long, and I sent my suggestions out into cyberspace, hoping for just one little nibble.

Hi Stephanie,
Thanks for sending along some fiction suggestions. We just finished up our Sept/Oct issue, and due to space reasons, I had to move several reviews slated for Sept/Oct into the Nov/Dec issue. I don't have the need to assign any further reviews at this point.

*However, I'll definitely keep you in mind for our Jan/Feb 2007
issue.*
All best,

I was starting to feel like I had met a guy at a bar and after he
came onto me and gave me his number, his roommate always said he
wasn't at home.

I'd wanted to write for this magazine for so long, so I thought,
okay, don't give up now. It's just the process. Do what you have to
to get in. In November, I e-mailed her to say I was still interested in
contributing to the Jan/Feb issue.

Hi Stephanie,
*Thanks for checking in. We're still trying to wrap up our Jan/
Feb issue, but we'll be planning out March/April soon. Let me
know if you have any March/April titles you'd like to suggest for
review.*
All best,

No, not the titles again. I can't do this. But somehow I did.

Hi Stephanie,
*Thanks for the suggestions. One thing I need to point out is that
some of these books aren't March/April titles. We prefer to feature
books the month in which they're published, so review titles have
to be books that are coming out in March and/or April 2007.
With that in mind, do you want to put together another short
list?*
Best,

Isn't this like being hit by your spouse? You're supposed to walk
away the first time because you know it's not going to happen just
once. But you don't.

Getting titles for the month that the magazine is being published proved to be a whack of work. I went through page after page online and in magazines, searching for appropriate titles (there aren't as many as you'd think), and sent them off.

> *Hi Stephanie,*
> *Sorry it's taken me a while to get back to you . . . are you still interested in writing a review for the March/April issue? If so, how about a 300-word review on Kurt Andersen's* Heyday*? The review will be due by January 4. Let me know if you're interested and I'll send a contract next week.*
>
> *Also, I don't have a galley for this title, so you'll need to request one from the publisher.*
> *All best,*

Am I still interested? I'm about to lose my mind over here, lady. *Of course I'm still interested.* But now I had to go to the publisher to get a copy. In my almost decade of doing book reviews for numerous publications, I'd never had to get my own copy. I felt like I was in a very unhealthy relationship. I wanted to get out but I'd already invested all of this time and energy into it . . .

I received an e-mail from the book publisher:

> *Hi there,*
> *Please be advised that the title* Heyday *is not available until March 6, 2007. Please send your request closer to that date and we will be more than happy to send you a copy of the book.*
> *All the best,*

I e-mailed the magazine editor back to ask for another title. She asked me to pick one from the galleys I had. I didn't have any galleys. I had not yet been sent books at random by publishers.[3] I was not a magazine editor. I was a *freelance writer.* We don't get anything.

On December 12, the editor gave me a title that she would send out to me. She wanted me to have the review in to her on January 5.

I made my deadline.

On January 17, I received an e-mail saying that the magazine would no longer be published. There were instructions on how to get paid. I was paid for the piece, but the last issue was the one before the issue with my review. It took over half a year for me to go through hell and I didn't even get the satisfaction of seeing it in print.

Months later, I worked on a story about viewer discretions in television, in movies, and on radio. I had to make changes to it after the whole Justin/Janet debacle and then awaited publication so I could be paid — nine months later.

Nine months came and went and my check did arrive. But the story didn't get published because someone had done a similar story the month before and it included an interview with someone who mattered, so they used that one instead. The suck just keeps coming.

Getting into a Washington newspaper was exciting in and of itself, but *they* had contacted *me*. They had seen, somewhere, a story I did about the global fascination with Hello Kitty and wanted to run it on the front page of the Life section. *And* they were going to pay me a pretty good rate to boot. It was almost too good to be true. I did the few small edits that they asked for, sent it in, and waited for it to get published two weeks later. And . . . I got an e-mail stating that the paper was folding, but the story would still run, and I would still be paid. Where could they send the check?

I was brokenhearted. This was going to be a big boost to my career — something to really be proud of. The check arrived and I cashed it, but it wasn't as exciting as getting to see it in print. Sadly, I never did because the paper folded, and the editor left, and no matter who I called or e-mailed, a copy was never sent my way. So if anyone has a copy of that last issue of the *Washington Asia Press* newspaper . . .

---

[3] This will happen in less than a year and I will end up with roughly 75 books, all of which I'm to read and review.

Back in the '90s I got a call from *The Oprah Winfrey Show.*[4] Oh yes, *that* Oprah.

I had sent a letter to an author who was to appear on the show (unbeknownst to me) and it ended up in the hands of Oprah and her peeps. They called me at my parents' house (I had since moved out but had written the letter back when I was at home) and left a message on the answering machine — a clunky brown and black GE that used *microcassettes.* (Kids, ask your parental units about these. And while you're at it, get them to tell you about the $900 BetaMax they bought, and the microwave oven the size of the Hindenburg. Actually . . . get 'em to tell you about the Hindenburg too. . . .) Messages were always accompanied by a loud hiss, no matter what you did with that rough-edged volume wheel.

I think it was Gayle (yes, *that* Gayle) who left the message, or maybe one of Gayle's assistants. They told me they wanted me to come out to tape a segment, and could I come out the day after next?

I pressed stop and played the message two more times just to make sure I had heard them right, and that I wasn't suddenly being transported to some alternative universe where a girl who looked exactly like me was getting a call from Oprah's people.

My hands shook as I took down the 1-800 number that they asked me to call back "as soon as possible," to confirm I could go.

The only thing I could think of as I was dialing the number was what I could possibly wear to such a life-changing event. Does one wear silk? Probably fur, right?

But because this was the early '90s, a lot of 1-800 numbers only worked in certain areas and often didn't work outside of the U.S. When I tried to return the call, I kept getting an automated message saying that I was outside the calling area: "Your call cannot be completed."

I was devastated and not sure what to do. I didn't yet have a computer or e-mail and I didn't know how to even fax them — what

---

[4] This was when she was popular, but had not yet taken over the world. This was pre–Oprah Book Club Oprah, Oprah Angel Network Oprah, *O* Oprah, etc.

a different and much simpler time that was.

I paced and panicked, held my stomach, and pulled my fingers through my hair. I decided that all I could do was wait for them to call back.

They called back the next day but *while I was at work.* They left the same "toll-free" number and when I tried it again, it still could not be completed.

They never called back and the show went on. Without me. I'd come *this* close to being on *The Oprah Winfrey Show* because of something I wrote.

I guess it's better than nothing.

the vagina song

MANY YEARS AGO, I was a book and music critic for PopMatters.com, which still today holds up in the glut of culture sites. It was during my time there that I reviewed a book called *The Camera My Mother Gave Me* by Susanna Kaysen. As I wrote back then, "Famous for *Girl, Interrupted,* she is someone whose autobiographical material fills volumes. Me, I have nothing."

This book is a memoir about a mysterious vaginal pain that the author endured for a year. Part of my review read:

Ahem. I don't know how to say this other than to be blunt — this book is about vaginas. Well, not a whole whack of them. Just one. Susanna's. Yep. She wrote an entire book about it. Now granted, she did (maybe still does) have a condition and perhaps this will go on to help all those women out there with burning, bumpy V's, but I can't imagine this being a very popular Christmas gift this year. When you pass a book along, it says not only something about you but also about the person you give it to. What could you possibly think of your friend if you gave her this (unless of course she had a burning, bumpy V)?

I called the review *Vagina Monologue*, which — for a girl like me who sucks at titles — wasn't too bad.

I thought it was funny and forgot about it.

In order to post my work on my website, I have to Google myself every week to see what links have come up. I write for so many magazines and websites with varying lead times that this is the only way in which to keep track. Weird, I know, but it's worked so far.

So I Googled myself and all of sudden, my Kaysen review had been picked up by porn websites. And not just a couple. *A lot.* A couple pages worth of links.

The first thing I thought of was, "Great. There goes my credibility as a journalist." I started to worry that people would think I'm a porn writer.

Now, I have nothing against people writing it, doing it, or enjoying it, but I have spent my life trying to be an upstanding citizen that my parents could be proud of. Porn was a venture that I had stayed away from, along with phone sex work, stripping, and general debauchery, except those few years in my late teens and early twenties when I danced my ass off at clubs into the wee hours of the morning. But I was fully clothed, and really, that's not that bad when you think about it.

However, I was pretty sure that no one would notice (who would be Googling me except for me?), and that it was just a misunderstanding and would dissipate quickly.

I was swamped with deadlines, so I forgot about it for a while. When it was time to update my website again, I went online to find that the couple of pages of porn sites that had ripped off my review had quadrupled. Now there was no doubting that I was the queen of porn, and people would soon be showing up at my house with cameras and various pleather accessories.

The problem persisted because I didn't want to go to the actual porn sites to see my piece. I was worried that somehow porn spam would infiltrate my lovely computer, which is my life and my work. Up until now, the only slightly naughty JPEG I had was an Abercrombie & Fitch ad of shirtless men in jeans laughing and running through a field.

I considered calling up a lawyer (I didn't have one because we hadn't got married, bought a house, or ever been in trouble) but was afraid that I would forever be formally known as a porn scribe. I hemmed and hawed for a couple of months, while the number of sites and links multiplied like Joan Rivers's facelifts. I was doomed, I thought.

Finally, I caved, and went to one of the sites to try to find an e-mail address where I could write to and ask them to remove my review.

After ten minutes of learning that apparently everything is up for grabs when it comes to fetishes, and that, curiously, neighbors are all the rage (ew), I could not find an e-mail address or webmaster — just a mistress named Jane and a whole bunch of handlebar-mustached men (double ew).

Thankfully, I was a member of Access Copyright. Membership is free and they provide "users with the ability to copy from millions of copyright protected materials while ensuring creators and publishers are fairly compensated." They also provided me with someone who figured out how to get to the porn webmasters and their legions of folks with their pants around their ankles. After about six months, it all went away, and I was just a regular girl writing about the latest disc from 10 Watt Mary and the state of the arts in Canada.

However, when I titled my next piece "Pulp Friction" . . .

one thing
leads to another

IT'S WEIRD when I meet another writer because often this means they're my competition. You don't want to wish them ill, but at the same time, you want to be able to make the rent.

One thing you'll quickly learn is how small the writing community is. A poet I had long admired contributed to a magazine where I eventually became an editor. There was a launch party and I was introduced to her quickly, but never got to say more than "Hell—" before I was pulled away for something else. A couple of years later she was at an '80s a cappella night and finally I got to tell her that I loved her work. As soon as I had just finished the "erk" part of the sentence, I was yanked away to be introduced to someone (apparently people can't wait to show me things).

I couldn't believe how great she looked. She had India ink hair done up Bettie Page–style. Smart and beautiful. It can happen.

Years went by, I filled out and eventually left my job to pursue writing full-time. Because my time was now my own, I fulfilled my dream to work at the Toronto Film Festival (most people dream of fame and fortune — I dreamed of working at the busiest, craziest movie box office for ten days). On the first day of training, a mahogany-haired woman sat next to me and we waited for the supervisors to finish roll call.

"Jennifer."

The girl beside me called out "yes."

I hadn't recognized her one bit.

I tapped her on the shoulder and explained how long I'd been following her work. She laughed and we talked while the people in charge said important things about procedures that we would live and die by ten days later.

I ended up covering her shift at a theater one night and we eventually became friends and compadres.

About nine months later, I applied to host a local volunteer radio program one hour a week. It focused on interviewing artists, authors, and musicians, all of which I had ample experience at. It was a little more indie and underground than I was, though if you consider how many mainstream magazines I *wasn't* getting into, I was pretty indie. The decision would be announced via e-mail in six weeks. I did what all actors do after an audition — forgot about it. That way, if you don't get the job, you won't fall into depression, and if you do, you'll be pleasantly surprised. I went about my merry business of reviewing restaurants, slathering on various new products, and writing my little heart out about Rachel McAdams, the latest laptops, and creating a spa in your own bathroom.

Exactly six weeks later, the e-mail arrived to say that unfortunately, I did not make the cut (they put it more gently than that). They had found the perfect host in someone who was a big part of the scene already — Jennifer. I was thrilled for her as she was indeed the perfect choice, and I sent her an e-mail saying so. She couldn't believe she had got the position, and we laughed about going for the same stuff.

We were competing, but not really. She writes poetry and fiction, and is a fixture in indie mags and readings around the city. Jennifer was definitely the right person for the job.

And I am glad to finally be getting to know the woman behind the work. I know that whatever jobs we both go out for, it will end up going to the right gal — Jen wins all the wet T-shirt contest gigs while I prevail over the car spokesmodel posing, complete with fluid hands and thick, caked-on brows. I don't mind losing out to her one bit.

My friends who write full-time in whatever realm — be it the travel columnist at the paper, the crime-writing novelist who finishes books within the year by only eking out a couple hours a day, or the handsome screenwriter in my living room — inspire me because somehow they have managed to do it for themselves too. I want to write books in a year and have seven newspaper columns going at once — not instead of them, but *beside* them, cheering them on as they celebrate my successes and I theirs.

However, when bad writers get the jobs because of who their parents are? Well, that makes me wanna throw up.

You know who you are. And so do the rest of us.

You're not fooling anyone.

lifestyles of
the rich and famous

CELEBRITIES ARE as much a part of our daily lives as brushing our teeth. They not only inhabit trashy tabloids, but have become the thrust of mainstream magazines and newspapers everywhere. Because of the star-driven culture we live in, you are aware of artists in ways you weren't before. Even your boss knows who Nicole Richie is, and your mother and my mother know that Tara Reid (of such classy shows as *Taradise* and *Body Shots*) is only known for her partying, no matter how many press conferences she holds to infer otherwise.

And while the stars of the '40s were followed by paparazzi and featured on magazine covers, they were not run down outside of their home by swarms of photographers vying to get the shot. They did not have their own clothing lines, and were certainly not known for their sex tapes, club antics, and/or their association with certain gangstas.

Whether you want to know about them or not doesn't seem to matter at all these days. The fact that I have only ever seen one episode of *The O.C.* has not barred me from knowing the names of at least four cast members (Adam Brody, Mischa Barton, Peter Gallagher, and Rachel Bilson). Nor is it strange that I know all the fellas in Green Day have kids. This is just stuff you pick up, even if you only read *Time* and *Newsweek*. But I am not ashamed to be fascinated by January Jones's perpetually sexy, tousled persona that is neatly packaged into Betty Draper on AMC's *Mad Men*, by the appearance of *The Office* actors in *License to Wed*, and, because I am only human, by Jin's cheekbones and Sawyer's stomach on *Lost*. I know things about celebrities that I have yet to find out about in friends that I have had for the past decade. That's just how it is.

One of the things that we can't seem to get enough of as a society is seeing celebrities do things like us normal folks: grocery shopping, filling their cars up with gas, and going to the local Starbucks for their daily caffeine fix. Despite the designer clothes, limo drivers, and extravagant houses, a lot of them just seem to try to raise their kids, have decent relationships, and do work that happens to be public.

Of course, there are those who would do just about anything to be sure to get into the next issue of *In Touch*. But the celebrities I have interviewed have all been quite decent, thoughtful human beings. Maybe I've just been lucky. I haven't had to interview Paris Hilton, Phil Spector, or Pete Doherty yet.

I am not like some of the writers in my city who get an assignment from a big glossy magazine, get paid thousands of dollars for it, and then get called just after it's been published to work on something else for an even higher-profile magazine. Although I have been at this a decade, I am not there. *Yet.* One reason is that I don't know the right people. Being in certain circles and knowing someone at a publication can move you ahead like nothing else. I go to events and parties and try to "network," but really what I end up doing is having a drink and finding out what *other* people are doing.

It is hard finding a balance between getting the "big stories" — an interview with the au courant celebrity, or writing about expensive cars or real estate for a five-page full-color spread — and the stuff that matters to you personally. It's about finding those stories that move you, yet still bring in the Benjamins. I'm still looking for that balance. I'm off to write about how to store beets and what to do to protect your hair from sun damage.

But tomorrow, who knows? Perhaps that Brad Pitt interview will land in my lap after all.

all these things that i've done

"I am always doing things I can't do, that's how I get to do them."
— Pablo Picasso

I HAVE FEW regrets in life, but one is not taking typing class.

For most kids at high school, typing is an easy credit and most, I think, figure it will come in handy one day. I saw it as a dead end, an assurance that I would end up being an assistant somewhere, doing nothing but paperwork (what ironically most of my office jobs consisted of). This was back when the Commodore 64 was the high-tech computer of choice. The computers in the schools used punch cards and were left for the science nerds, and in 1983, we kids certainly didn't have the foresight to envision being on computers all day long like we are now. Though we did think we'd be driving hovercrafts.

So while I didn't take typing, I somehow managed to work in offices with my special version of typing, which had my fingers flying over the keys in a jagged, staccato symphony. It became a problem when I'd have to do dictation and I didn't automatically know where the keys were. I knew the area in which they were, but the lawyer I worked for, and later some doctors, barked out the correspondence so quickly that I kept my head down and then made the changes later when they left the room.

It also became a problem when I had to type things extremely quickly, like manuscripts or larger documents. While I had an amenable speed for a self-taught typist, I was not a whiz like the full-time office manager I worked for. Without ever glancing at the keys, Victoria could type a full-page document with incredible speed and accuracy using just the tips of her long nails while talking on the phone and motioning for a patient to go on in and see the doctor. She is still the fastest typist I know.

I swore that I had to learn how to type properly so that I could work faster. I was always looking out for anything to speed up my efficiency — this certainly would be a big help.

So I found an online program that had you work small groups of keys first, the middle line, then the bottom and top. You were timed and could only move onto the next level if you got a certain score based on your speed. It took me about three months to get it right, then another three months of a mash-up style of my old ways mixing with the new.

I now use only the traditional method I learned online, but I'm just about as fast as I was doing my own thing. I never look at the keys anymore though, which is something. I imagine in a year or two, I'll be up to a speed that I think respectable. Not Victoria-fast, but fast.

One of the other things I had been dying to do was take a non-fiction writing class.

Non-fiction is a funny place to hone your skills because everyone assumes that if you are a writer, you have a novel in you, that you write short stories and you spend your days creating woolly characters who get up to no good. I took a fiction writing class online once and wrote half a novel about a group of twentysomething friends navigating their way through careers and relationships. It was awful;

I hope I don't have the notes anywhere anymore. The teacher loved it though, and I imagine that it was the same kind of thing that is now popular among the mainstream crowd that loved the Sophie Kinsella books and anything pink with a punny title about relationships, which remain high on the best-seller charts.

I didn't finish the course because I knew my creative writing sucked and it wasn't what I wanted to do. I wanted to conduct interviews, do research, and create rich, full-bodied pieces that would inform and entertain readers. I have always been a non-fiction writer and can't imagine a time when I could be anything else.

When I started out, not too long ago, there weren't many writers who just wrote non-fiction. I sought out as many as I could in the small bunch and came up with some excellent examples of folks who had created a style all their own and inspired me — that they had done it and done it so well meant to me that there was a small possibility that I too could do it if I just worked at it hard enough. Now there are *tons* of them.

Chris, my former editor at a writing magazine, had recently moved into my neighborhood and we'd started hanging out. It turned out that we both loved books and cooking and so we'd get together at a local stomping ground and talk about where to get the best fish and what essay was gripping us at the moment. Chris was very encouraging when I was at the magazine and on the day before it went under, he bestowed upon me the title of assistant editor, one that, though it might have been name alone, meant a great deal to me.

His best friend, Degan, had a great fiction course that he taught at university and had adapted into an e-mail course for Chris. I had mentioned that I wished to God someone would make a non-fiction one already and he said that he thought his friend had one too.

Degan had indeed crafted his course into a non-fiction one, and despite not really making any money at writing so far, I was so excited to have found someone who knew what non-fiction was about. I asked Scott if we could eat a lot of pasta in the next month or two, and began a course that would change my writing forever.

Degan understood my writing in a way no one had before. It's like when you meet someone and they love that same obscure band that you do and know all of their intricacies: you become so close instantaneously. I hadn't met Degan, but through e-mails and his notes on my weekly assignments, we forged a relationship that I have found in only a few people and for which I am deeply grateful. He forced me to really look at the words I chose and how I was describing things. I write pretty quickly and get it out because otherwise I would never finish anything. Laboring over words and paragraphs was one of the most difficult encounters I've ever had — but entirely worth it. After his specially designed ten-lesson course, I felt like I'd finally done some writing I was damn proud of.

And now I can get it all down in half the time, thanks to my new typing skills.

Next on the list — a meat-butchering course, getting my driver's license (hey, I grew up in the city) and my own columns in *New York*, *Esquire*, *GQ*, and *The New Yorker*.

this is how we do it

"I do like to read a book while having sex. And talk on the phone. You can get so much done."
— Movie star Jennifer Connelly, quoted in the *Atlantic* magazine

I AM SO GOOD at multitasking that if there were an *Iron Chef* show for doing eight things at once, I'd win hands down. *Banzai!*

I can be making dinner, have laundry in, be researching a topic for an article, talking to someone on the phone, and sending an e-mail, all at the same time. No problem. Thanks to my new cell phone with full keyboard, subway rides have turned into another opportunity to complete tasks, answer e-mail, edit an article, or start writing something new.

Of course, in the second year of writing full-time, this had led to disaster. So much so that before leaving for vacation, I was so overwhelmed by what I needed to do that despite my many lists to follow and check off, I would find myself in the middle of the kitchen, standing with the fridge open, or downstairs at the mailbox, unable to recollect the last five minutes, how I got there, and why I was there at all.

My brain had been on overload for months and I was scrambling just to keep up. I was still meeting my deadlines, but barely. I couldn't focus on anything and my writing, sleep, and pretty much everything suffered.

Fresh from a vacation in the Dominican Republic — where all that was scheduled for my day was aerobics in the pool and dinner at the "Italian" restaurant — I was finally able to think clearly again and realized I had slipped into the old multitasking habit. Despite knowing its trappings, I again went into full attack mode and tried to do it all.

I am now trying the ol' do-one-thing-at-a-time mode, though I do relapse every once in a while. I mean, who doesn't listen to their iPod while watching TV and working?

Just kidding. I don't do that. But I do listen to my MP3 player while typing on my computer, which is linked to my smartphone that I update while my computer is uploading, downloading, or while I am searching for a word. And did I mention that I've also got a pot of stew simmering on the stove?

It's a little different than the world my parents live in. I love 'em to death, but up until about five years ago, they still had the black rotary dial phone and bleary answering machine with a miniature tape left over from my first apartment. They've come a long way recently. They have a fax, iMac, and cordless phones — though there is still confusion among them between cell and cordless phones. Every once in a while, my mom wonders if she has to pay for airtime for the cordless and forgets that she is not bound by a tangly cord, that she can actually walk around.

According to an article in *Wired*, "Multitasking can release stress hormones that hamper job performance and may eventually lead to depression, anxiety, and amnesia. Take breaks, eat well, exercise, and be sure to get enough sleep."

I read endless articles about how the last decades of multitasking were just a façade of the busy worker and how it's all about doing one thing at a time now. It feels awfully like the whole coffee, eggs, and beef are good/bad for you debate that has been going on for my entire existence.

So while I do try to be completely present for time periods when I'm working on my book or hunkering down to finish a restaurant review, I am usually testing perfumes while cleaning the tub, then hopping up to research an article about flying comfortably and chop veggies for dinner, all in a matter of a few minutes.

things i am supposed to do this week

- Follow up on outstanding invoices
- Call four chefs to interview
- Make photocopies
- Pick up stamps
- Get birthday presents for Darren, Eddie, Alan, and Shelley
- Return books to the library
- Call and make appointment for annual physical
- Go to bank
- Plan this week out and next week with action lists
- Review my calendar
- Back up my documents, music, pictures, e-mail, and book manuscript
- Update my website
- Write tomorrow's blog post and get accompanying picture
- Virus scan my computer
- Erase all of the voice mails that have piled up
- Write four articles for a food magazine
- Pitch computer magazine
- Pitch spa magazine
- Make notes on new ideas
- Work on book
- Organize tax papers
- Pay bills
- Prep for telephone interview with R&B singer Jully Black — research online and in print to prep for interview, get her CDs, and listen to them at least three times
- Read book for review
- Write up review
- Research and write article on food and nutrition
- Try out fitness shoes that are supposed to trim your thighs
- Try out new skin-care line — scrub, mask, cleanser, clay mask, day cream, night cream, eye cream, neck cream, toner

I know that I should be centering myself more, taking up meditation and focusing on the here and now. But technology and the speed at which I can get information has ruined me for good: I finished the previous paragraph at 8:17 P.M. Before tucking into bed at 11:30, I did the dinner dishes, mopped the kitchen floor, created this week's to-do list of e-mails, calls, and errands, wrote three thank-you cards, wrapped two birthday presents, picked a movie to see tomorrow night, toggled between updating my website and posting a blog (I'm not spending my life watching that green bar fill up), and worked on a chapter of this book.

This, of course, pales in comparison to Ms. Connelly.

wrapped up in books

"MERRY CHRISTMAS, pumpkin."

My dad hands me a square package wrapped in three-month-old newspaper, with every edge covered with both masking and silver duct tape, leaving no edge undone.

"Thanks, Pa."

I get up and go into my kitchen for a pair of scissors that I keep in the utensil drawer to the left of the sink. I come back to the couch and get to cutting and ripping and tearing.

Two minutes later, the title of the book (because it could be nothing else but a book, it is *always* a book) is revealed. A sharp intake of breath.

The Best of S. J. Perelman. And not just any copy, but *his* copy.

I look up and all I can push out of my mouth is "Pa . . ."

His ropey hand goes to his tumbleweed of a beard. He strokes it with his bandaged fingers (always two) that are smeared with ink and grimy fingernails.

"He's a really good writer, so I thought you should have him on your shelf."

We are both overcome with emotion, and yet the moment doesn't allow for more than a few words.

"It's a good read."

"Thanks, Pa."

tongue like
a battering ram

MOST OF MY writing career has been about describing things.

But it started long before that. I would think about how to describe a caramel, knee-length sheepskin coat I saw on someone on Queen West, or the hair of an Afghan dog. It became a personal challenge that somehow along the way became a career choice.

And I am completely enthralled when I read someone who can really do it well, like this from Marisha Pessl's *Special Topics in Calamity Physics*:

> The few pieces of humble furniture — chest of drawers, wooden Quaker chair, a vanity table — had been relegated to the corners of the room as if they'd been punished. The bed was queen sized, neatly made (although where I was sitting it wrinkled) and the comforter (or bedspread, as there was nothing comforting about it) was a thorny blanket the color of brown rice. The bedside table featured a lamp, and on the bottom shelf only a single well-worn book, *I Ching*,

or *The Book of Changes*. ("There's nothing more irritating than Americans hoping to locate their inner Tao," Dad said.) Standing up, I noticed a faint but unmistakable smell hanging in the air, like a flashy guest that refused to go home: men's musky cologne, the sort of persistent syrup a Miami hunk doused on his truck-thick neck.

Now *that's* description.

I can write a feature article in an hour or two, but reviews can take three times as long, simply because of the amount of careful description involved. When I was writing about music, I'd listen to a song and really try to describe the pings and wahs so that if you'd never heard the band or song before, you'd get a sense of what they sounded like, what they were trying to do. Book reviews are very similar, though it takes a heckuva long time because you have to read the freakin' book first. And restaurant reviews are the same thing, only more difficult. I try very hard to write to everyone — both the foodie and the novice — so my vocabulary can't be too exclusive. If you've never heard of sorrel, gnudi, or argon oil, then I'd better make it clear what it is. I spend a ridiculous amount of time at my desk trying to come up with words to describe the food.

Restaurant reviews are difficult because I don't want them all to be a formula of "Here's the décor, the wine list selection, and what I had to eat." I try to make each one different, though those weeks that I visit three Italian restaurants back-to-back are tough — I mean, how many different ways are there to prepare veal parmigiana? Right. Now try to describe them all without being repetitive. It's enough to make me want to throw in the towel and go to circus school.

The time I spend on restaurant reviews isn't just trying to find another way to write "savory" though. It's the time it takes to incorporate my notes into the actual review. I interview the chef and/or owner for the piece, which means I spend most of my time there taking notes, handwriting them in hardcover notebooks, and then referring back to them when writing up the piece. I tried recording them at first, but you have to transcribe everything, so it ends up being twice as much work in the end. (Every once in a while I get fed up and try to find a transcriber, but there aren't many, and they are damn expensive. Usually as much or more than I'm getting for the piece. Besides, in order to do the piece, I need those transcriptions *right now* because my deadline is in two days.) So now I write everything down very quickly while I'm at the restaurant, then pluck out what I need when I'm writing up the piece. This is the best system I've come up with so far.

The only problem is my handwriting. My handwriting is so bad that my own mother has to call me when I've sent her a card to go over what I wrote — why did I take my couch down the Danforth and what was Bob Newhart doing in the laundry room? And when the neighbors got our postcards from the Dominican, they came over and had about seventy-five percent of it worked out.

The weird thing about taking notes during an interview — whether it's a chef or a celebrity — is that they watch everything you write. And quite often, men will ask me, "Did you get that last part down? Lemme see."

You're not seeing anything, mister. Do I come in and root around your chicken soup making sure the mirepoix ratio is correct?

I don't think so.

So sometimes it takes me up to ten minutes to figure out a word I wrote down that someone said. It's annoying but it's the best system I've come up with. If you have a better one, believe me, I'm all ears.

Between deciphering my own handwriting, trying to piece together a review from quotes, my own observations, and astute recollections of the food, they take a heck of a long time.

And although sometimes I am so frustrated, I want to crash my J.T. CD against the wall (Never, Justin. *Never!*), I do enjoy the challenge of it.

Restaurant and music reviews are the hardest writing I've come across. But I'll keep at it because there is such a thrill in finding that perfect word or sentence to describe something. When it is bang on, you know it. What a feeling!

The thing about reviewing is that if you like a certain thing

— listening to music, reading, eating — reviewing seems like the perfect job. You're doing these things anyway, why not get paid for it? Well, the thing is, I have yet to get a really sweet paying reviewing gig. (To all of my editors: I am eternally grateful to be working for you, and by no means am I complaining about the size of the checks you send me.) Book reviewing pays poorly, unless you are Stephen King sputtering out wisdom on the back page of *Entertainment Weekly*.

I used to write for free when I first started just to get the experience, to keep writing to deadline, and to get my feet wet in different markets, doing different kinds of writing. I know this is controversial to some, and that some folks can do all of that while raking in money writing. I don't regret all that time spent because I learned so much about writing, and about myself along the way. It was definitely worth the trip.

But I don't write for free anymore. I knew that I'd reach a point where I'd stop and it feels good to have passed into the next level where people assume that I only work for money. It feels damn good. And this way, we can get that organic coffee that we like so much without having to mortgage the house.

However, all that being said, I still do book reviews for a measly amount. I have yet to crash into the market of $500 book reviews. (I assume this is what Updike and that guy who wrote that book about the Mormons and the mountain get.) I write for scholarly journals and trade publications, and get the wee checks in the mail. I do it because I enjoy the work. It is challenging and I often get the opportunity to read things way out of my usual range.

Speaking of ranges, I wrote a review of a book about *The Gunslinger*, a short-lived Western show that aired in 1961. It starred Ron Hagerthy and was very much of the time. In fact, reading about the "injuns," and "whores," and whipping dogs for misbehaving was extremely troubling.[5]

But it wasn't just reading about the show's content that was difficult. It was the critique of a show that I had never seen, and I had to

---

[5] Remember my reaction to *Benji*?

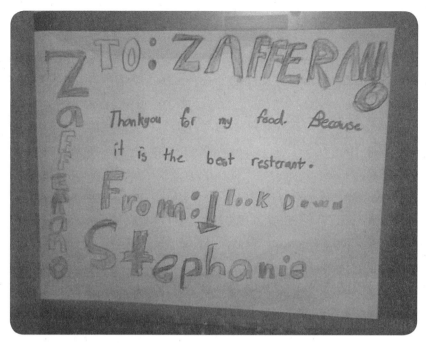

To: ZAFFERN
Thankyou for my food. Because it is the best restarant.
From: ↓ look Down
Stephanie

I finally get a great reviewing gig and another Stephanie has to horn in.

critique the critique. That, and it was about Westerns, which are just about the most loathsome subject I can imagine watching (except you, Brad Pitt, in *The Assassination of Jesse James*. You, mister, changed my thoughts about cowboys forever).

So it took me night after night struggling to read this book about a subject that was of little interest and with offensive content about a show I've never seen. It was like trying to sit through a movie starring Carrot Top.

The book wasn't long by any means, but it took me a week to get through it and I felt completely drained by the end. I wrote the piece and struggled some more, hoping that I sounded academic enough. I sent it off with a huge sigh and hoped that I never had to do anything like that again.

I got an e-mail back saying thanks, there are no changes, and the review will be out in two and a half years.

Wha?

That is the longest lead time I've ever had to wait. And remember folks, I get paid *upon publication.*

So now I am still waiting for it to come out, to see what I wrote (I often see something I did months prior and if it weren't for my name beside the piece, I wouldn't know it was mine), and, you know, to get paid.

In my career, there are often these kinds of assignments where I scuffle my way through, just barely making it. And it is such a relief to get them done.

But it's not always horrible. Sometimes I get assigned books that really do change my life, where I seek out more titles by the author, and I'll write to them and say what a grand work they've created. Reading books can be so powerful it can set me off on a course that otherwise I would not have taken. It's not always (almost never in fact) those titles that you think will rock your world. It's those innocuous ones that just creep up on you, and all of a sudden you can't wait to go to bed to read more, and you find yourself constantly talking about finding this gem. It is such an amazing feeling that when I get a review book that does this, getting paid on top of it is like winning the lottery — you're going to introduce me to this book *and* pay me?

And that is why I have the maximum number of books out at my library (fifty) and the maximum holds (fifty). Although I certainly don't get to them all, I do breeze through almost all of them. I have found authors that totally knock my socks off, and books that were so amazing that I still talk about them years later, like great boy-friends who introduced me to Brazilian hip-hop, Paul Bowles, and French documentaries.

Reviewing books is like getting paid for the opportunity to discover new folks and stories that embed themselves in me.

For *The Writer*, I get to read books on writing, which I think is important for me. It reminds me of little things I could be doing, and in some cases, what *not* to do. Even the books that aren't great are valuable in that I learn what to avoid and how to be better. It is like taking a writing class and getting paid for it, and then being able to educate others about it.

As a professional writer, however, I'm noticing book review pages are disappearing. Newspapers, definitely. Magazines, almost certainly. So there are not a lot of places for me to go that will pay me to read. This will require some more serious digging on my part.

In the meantime, I'll be over there in that chair. The one with the piles of books beside it.

catch me while I'm sleeping

ONE OF THE THINGS that no one told me about the writing life is how tiring it is. And it doesn't matter if you are racing to interview an author and then fighting rush-hour traffic to get home because you then have to transcribe it and turn it into interesting copy all in matter of hours, or if you are merely sitting on the couch reading a book that you have to review and have on the editor's desk in three days.

They are both exhausting.

I get to my desk early-ish — between six and eight, depending on the evening before. My desk is just a few feet from our bed, which surprisingly doesn't factor into the sleepiness that comes with the job. And like I used to when I worked in an office, I shower, dress, and get coffee all before sitting down at my desk.

I used to have just a coffee and a half throughout the day, but it seems that it is not nearly enough to keep me going anymore. I switch to black teas, ginseng drinks, and various sodas in order to keep up the momentum. But no matter what I do or how early I get up, by 2 p.m. I am so sleepy that I just want to curl up and have a one- or two-hour nap. And I'm my boss, so I certainly could. No one would know. But I just can't. There are so many hours in the day and I really do want to make the most of them.

7 a.m. — Making notes and answering e-mail: 1½ coffee

8 a.m. — Writing up restaurant review: 1 black tea

9:30 a.m. — E-mailing editor about cover story and interview: second black tea

10:00 a.m. — Go get the mail. Disappointed that I haven't won the Reader's Digest Lottery, that apparently Ed McMahon doesn't even have time to write anymore, and that although it seems that I just paid rent, it is that time again.

10:08 a.m. — Too depressed to drink anything.

10:21 a.m. — I get an e-mail reminding me that my piece is due tomorrow. I had thought it was the 21st of *next* month. Fuuuuuuuuuuuuuck.

10:22 a.m. — Sheer panic. Fingers flying on the keyboard. Two coffees lined up and consumed so quickly that tonight I will not be able to taste the chicken because my mouth is burned almost raw.

1:49 p.m. — The piece is finished and I am exhausted. Time to take a lunch break.

2:01 p.m. — I sit down on the couch in the living room, have my soup and salad and a cup of tea, and read an article from one of the magazines out of the Pisa-like tower beside the couch.

2:19 p.m. — I am finished lunch and see my review book glaring at me through the glass door of the bookshelf. It's due in three days. I should get started.

2:23 p.m. — I have yawned every forty-five seconds for the last four minutes. I start to wonder if I have sleep apnea or something. I make a note to get those nose strips that help you breathe at night. Maybe that will help.

2:25 p.m. — I start a book about a guy in prison who's also time-traveling. Oh great. This isn't going to take long at all. Uggggggggh.

2:43 p.m. — I am on page 19 and I want to shoot myself. I am also struggling to stay awake. I now have my head on the couch

I swear this is work.

pillow and am outstretched. It is so comfortable and yet this book is sooo slow. I will carry on though. I am a consummate professional.

2:43:03 P.M. — I am asleep. Drool covers the pillow. Cosmo's curled up on my chest.

4:04 P.M. — Scott comes through the front door and I sit up in that sleepy daze that leaves you half in dream state and strikingly in the present.

"Were you asleep?"

"Nope. No, I'm working. Reading a review book. Yep. It's going well. Lotsa work."

I casually place my book on the drooly pillow. No one ever has to know.

i woke up with this song in my head this morning

"Without music, life would be a mistake."

— Friedrich Nietzsche

YOGA MATS SLUNG over the shoulders of slim-hipped girls with glossy ponytails, nu-metal tank tops, and tattoos that spell "creative" and "balance" in careful Chinese lettering. Faux-hawked men underneath headphones the size of saucers, with the hiss of bass seeping into the air.

The world has changed a lot in the last decade. Especially in the last year. And that can been seen in music more than anywhere else — film, books, even fashion. The explosion of music genres is as swift as Rihanna's costume changes and Victoria Beckham's haircuts. I am not the only one who feels left behind. Remember the days when Snoop was known by his full name, there was a section called "Country and Western," and you listened to a CD *all the way through*?

Writing for music websites and publications, I quickly realized how incredibly hard it is to keep up not only with the sheer volume of bands and artists being represented, but with new genres being created on a seemingly daily basis.

I could not keep track of the latest bands and I was *in the know*. Each month there are thirty that have "taken the music world by storm." Trying to understand not only who Yellowcard, Slum Village, Atreyu, Switchfoot, Pocket Dwellers, Boys Night Out, and RJD2 were, but then trying to figure out which music category they fell into was like being in university — my desk became a pile of books, magazines, and reams of printouts off the Net. I became obsessed with trying to stay up-to-date. Earphones became a permanent affixation. I could hear a tribal beat in everything for a while there. From week to week, the music charts are changing so drastically that if you don't keep up, you can be let out of the loop in a month's time.

Consider the Pop genre. How did Gym Class Heroes, Diana Krall, Modest Mouse, and Barry Manilow manage to all fall under the same umbrella? Open up the Pop envelope and out falls Disco Pop, done by artists such as what *Rolling Stone* deems "*the* American band," the Scissor Sisters (say that fast three times). Then there's Electronica. This is the most frustrating. Unless you are a DJ or an expert in a particular music style, it is difficult to distinguish between such subgenres as Jungle Soul, Yob-House (huh?), and what the hell is Nu-Purple Funk? Where is Brian Eno when I need him? The man who brought us Ambient is nowhere to be found.[6] Is that Enya (I still consider her New Age, clearly showing my age) or Delirium?

I asked DJ and musician friends and no one could give me a straight answer. They pretended to know what Jump-Up and NuRNG were, but when pressed for definitions, everyone suddenly had bookshelves that needed dusting or dogs needing to be walked. Books are hopelessly outdated, magazines offer little guidance, and the Net is a glut of information that is hard to hone in on. Making it even more complicated is that what seems *in* one week, is already *out* just as it's becoming a hit. (See Black Eyed Peas' "My Humps" and white people still using "shizzle my nizzle" and "off the chain" while

---

[6] There is a constant rumor circulating that Brian Eno is doing a Roxy Music reunion. It is untrue. At least for now.

black people have clearly moved on already. Come on, Frankenberry. That is as played as Che Guevara T-shirts and Crocs.)

What's a girl to do? Radio is not the place to go anymore, and feverishly scouring the "record" stores each week and scrutinizing the latest music mags is too time-consuming, certainly if you are over nineteen. There is no way to keep up.

So I wanted to look into it deeper. I mean, I know I can't be the only one out there still trying to hear the nuance of difference between Bluegrass and New Grass. And what the hell is Dark Glitter anyway? Trying to categorize music these days is as difficult as it's going to be for Hayden Panettiere to do anything *without* the cheerleader costume. For instance, there's something called "Lifestyle Music" now. Described in a Coldplay article, "It's music that loft dwellers listen to as they sip chardonnay and eat risotto — stuff like Norah Jones and Dido." That's gonna start some fights between the music cognoscenti, let me tell you.

There used to be a great feature of the Listen.com site where they sent you a word from their glossary once a week. Some examples of music types that were featured are:

Dad rock (n.): Simply put, dad rock is music that your dad would enjoy. On a greater scale, this term encompasses a sense of warmth and security that only an acoustic guitar and some moccasins can provide. Dad rock hit its prime in the mid-'70s with artists like Bread and England and Dan & John Ford Coley. Dad rock makes you want to tuck in your shirt, put on a Henley-styled sweater with elbow pads, and just mellow out with your kids. Echoes of dad rock can be heard in the music of Paul Weller and Mojave 3.

Cheeseburger punk (n.): Numbskull rock 'n' roll, as created by Andy Shernoff of the Dictators. At a time when rock 'n' roll was becoming more and more outrageous (think Ziggy Stardust, Disco, the Eagles) and also more political, a few bands were going back to the essentials. The Ramones and the Dictators helped start a small but influential wave of music which embraced comic books, junk food, TV, B movies, professional wrestling, and other basics of the average teenager's life.

During all my years of being a music critic, I came across a lot of real genres that people might not be aware of. There are new genres that are really exciting. And while a bunch of folks might think that music today isn't like it *used to be,* I think it goes to show that new genres are always being developed and that musicians are straddling previously staid formats and categories.

Of course, people just making up genres makes it difficult. *Blender* magazine's genres have included Saddoes (music to cry over), Rawk (hit-you-in-the-ribs rock), Crunky (you don't want to know), and the self-explanatory Hipsters, Aging Hipsters, and Superstar Pop.

Sometimes, it's the musicians that make it difficult. Norah Jones calls her jazzy-poppy sound "Soft-Cock Rock." I don't think this is an official genre or subgenre, although you'd be surprised by the number of artists who qualify. Sexy Canadian rocker Sam Roberts spoke about his new album, *Chemical City,* with *Inside Entertainment* magazine. He called the album's sound "sci-fi Druid rock." Sam, you are so not helping. As to what the term means, I have no idea.

But maybe I'm just jealous that I didn't come up with it first.

please don't
stop the music

TIME MAGAZINE ONCE stated, "1972 — For the first measurable time in history, music is the most popular form of entertainment in America."

I think we just found our second time.

Investigating music's history is important as you can't know where you're going until you know where you've been. When researching articles and musicians for upcoming interviews, I was amazed at how far back and far ranging people's influences were. Eddie Van Halen looks to classical music while Zack de la Rocha of Rage Against the Machine claims Run-DMC and Charlie Parker as influences. Mike D of the Beastie Boys said, "For us, seeing Minor Threat at the CBGB hardcore matinee was just as necessary a force in our lives as the Treacherous Three at Club Negril, or the Funky Four + One More at the Rock Lounge."

This investigation led me to understand the fabric of our society much better. While some people may think music is superfluous, I believe it is as vital as anything else in our lives.

Rock on and keep it crunk.

One thing you can't fake is music knowledge. If you don't know who Broken Social Scene are, you can't just try to make your way through a conversation.

Music helps soften the feelings of alienation that accompany teenagehood and helps to define oneself. Knowing that a guy in your class "really gets" Death Cab for Cutie and knows the origin of their name (a song that was featured in *Magical Mystery Tour*, the Beatles movie) can change your life. At least for the moment. So whether you are a jock, Goth, stoner, cool kid, loner, drama geek, mathlete, or perhaps a former version of these, the music is gonna move you. And define you.

Interpreting music for yourself is another part of it. You are going for what you are innately attracted to, while trying to hold it up against what others think of it. You are always doing one of two things — either liking something because everyone else does, or else liking it because *no one else* does. It's as simple and as complicated as all that.

As a music critic (read: someone who gets paid to listen to and then write about music), I am expected to be the one friends turn to when they are looking to know what the latest Alesha Dixon disc is like, or whether Guru Josh Project is going to be releasing anything new soon. And whatever happened to Laura Branigan, or "Buffalo Stance" Neneh Cherry for that matter?

Herein lies the problem. Everyone over nineteen is extremely elitist about who they like. You can't go around yelling that you love "Don't Talk to Strangers" while wearing a T-shirt with "Jessie's Girl" emblazoned across your chest — unless you are doing it ironically, of course. It hasn't been cool to like Craig David — ever. Tsk. And if you even mention Billy Vera and the Beaters ("At This Moment"), Vince Gill, Dead or Alive, or Sister Sledge, you will quickly find yourself snubbed from conversation, like a Goth trying to intercept a circle of cheerleaders in the high-school cafeteria.

But more annoying are those who are so angry about it. The managing editor of *Chart* magazine, Canada's foremost music cognoscente, wrote a scathing piece on Pearl Jam and grunge. He said, "[T]he problem I have with Pearl Jam isn't actually with them. It's with what they spawned. As the purest distillate of grunge ideals, the PJs birthed countless imitators. Without Pearl Jam, discerning music fans wouldn't have had to suffer through Seven Mary Three or Stone Temple Pilots. Nor would there be Days of the New, Candlebox, Bush, Creed, or any of the many grungy roustabouts who still to this day assault my ears with their nonsensical grumble rock."

Ouch.

But I think it is time we brought back the love for music — *all* music. The music that I can't live without is otherwise embarrassing to those sitting next to me. But look to the musos, people. Chuck Klosterman's love for KISS is unapologetic. And I love that about him. He's giving his love *full-force*.

Even those for whom music is not a way of life, a certain judgment is made with every disc you buy, every song you claim is "it." It all comes down to belonging and taste (read: preference).

But there are some bands that you *have* to like. Why? Because *everyone* likes them. Like I know that I am *supposed* to like Coldplay. I just don't. Chris Martin's voice is just way too high and quivery for me. It's like he's always on the verge of crying, or something. You know, like James Blunt.

I can't tell you how much I want to, only so that I am not snuffed aside at parties. It is like not liking bananas or milk — how do you get *by* in this world?

And what is up with all the praise for R. Kelly? Review after review simply glows and I just don't get it. One person writing for the *iTunes Page-A-Day* calendar was completely swept away by "Happy People": "The beat is spare and sharp, and what's on top is simply luxurious: lithe guitars wah-wahing on the offbeat, subtle conga fills, sweeping strings, unobtrusive flute, and, crucially, a plethora of slightly differing vocal overdubs that give his soul-shouter side less room but make up for it in two-part harmonies that nag a little and cushion everywhere else."

To which I respond, *"HUH?!"*

Because I get to put my opinion in print, there is a certain credibility that gets lent to my name. And because I get to cover mainstream, up-and-coming, and indie groups, I can usually offer up a lot of suggestions of what to buy ("If you liked this, you might like this . . ."). However, this all falls apart when friends drop by the apartment and check out my own collection. Having pop music artists like Fergie, Eva Avila, and Kelly Clarkson nullifies my credibility with the supposed music "fiends." However, the titles they don't recognize don't get no respect either. These artists could be the next big thing, but because these supposed "experts" haven't seen the discs featured at HMV or heard them on the radio countdown, they are immediately discounted.

So, the so-called non-mainstreamers who are supposedly "all about the music" are upset about the mainstream discs that occupy part of my music shelf, but aren't willing to listen to the new stuff ("I've never heard of them, so how good can they be?"). Grrr. These are the same people who, in the safety of their own homes and in the privacy of their hard drives, spent three weekends in a row downloading Abba, Chicago, and Supertramp. Now there. I just used those bands as examples of lame music. There are going to be a whole whack of you that already have pen poised to paper, fingers trembling over keys, ready to scream at me. See how insidious it is?

Whatever happened to the issue of fun in music? Music to make you laugh, to dance to, to just enjoy it for what it is. When did liking music become so serious, where everyone is suddenly an expert? What about liking a nu-metal song because it is impossible not to nod your head to it? What about getting rid of all this shame and embarrassment?

I am tired for being made to feel bad for liking music outside of the elite's must-have list. This is not a contest for cool.[7] This is an

---

[7] Ben Stiller's List of Musical Influences for *Feel This Book*:
Music From *Miami Vice* — Various Artists
"Meaty Beaty Big and Bouncy" — The Who
John Tesh's Tour de France Score
"Dancing Machine" — Jackson 5
"Bad, Bad Leroy Brown" — Jim Croce
"Emotion" — Samantha Sang
"All You Need is Love" — The Beatles
"Eat My Foo Poppa Biddy Parts" — Pussmama G and the Furious 2

opportunity for finding your inner groove. And what could be more important than that?

Music can be the background sound that you listen to while doing other things — reading, vacuuming, working, or cooking. Or it can be a song or album that changed the course of your life.

Your choice.

But before you choose, you gotta listen to this . . .

daft punk is
playing at my house

REVIEWING MUSIC and interviewing singers sounds a lot more luxurious than it is.

Sure you get to keep the disc, and yes, you get to ask rappers those questions that have been burning your brain for the last six months, but believe me when I tell you that it is actually a lot of work.

Well, the way I do it anyway.

When I'm reviewing a disc, I research the person and their previous stuff to give me an added sense of where they've come from and where they're going.

Then I listen to the disc *at least* three times. I find that on the first listen, I can miss some of the essential tracks or be distracted by an interesting phrase or exceptionally catchy chorus. I always read — and finish — the books that I have for review and spend as much time as I can to really capture and then pass onto the reader my experience. How can you talk about something intelligently if you haven't finished it?

Then I try to figure out how to translate onto the page what it sounds like. This can take hours, even days depending upon how unfamiliar it is.

Scott tells me I take it *very* seriously and I guess I do.

I realize that many people will have a wildly different experience and may completely disagree with my methods, but my goal is to pass along my true feelings and experiences each and every time so that you know that when you're reading my stuff, you're getting my honest reaction and opinion.

Music is especially important as it is so woven into our lives. We all listen to it or used to, if you're too old for that stuff now (we remember you sock hoppin', potato mashin' fools in love and dancing the night away). It's everywhere — streaming live while you shop for jeans, in TV commercials (if I see or hear Feist one more time . . .), and blasting ass-dropping, window-thumping beats out of cars.

We all have songs and musicians that speak to us, that move us — sometimes to tears and sometimes onto the dance floor. You can tell a lot about a person by the music they listen to. And everyone's got an opinion — you can't talk about Chamillionaire or Bloc Party and think you'll get lukewarm responses. They're gonna get wild about it.

Music is seductive. It pulls you in. A song that really gets to you can cause you to sing or dance if you hear it at the mall or in the car next to you at a stoplight. I was waiting for a bus with my mom once and heard "Calabria 2007" seeping out of a Cutlass stopped at the light. I dropped my shopping bags and got down despite being the only person under the age of fifty-nine at the bus stop.

I write about music because it is difficult to describe and pinpoint, and yet so satisfying when you get it just right and someone who's never heard the track can practically hear it, thumping and rocking its way through their system.

That, and I can dance my ass off and call it "work."

by myself

BANDS WORK FOR months, often for years on a CD and then, somehow, it gets leaked onto the Internet. Some bands handle this better than others. A couple of years ago, this happened to Linkin Park, one of my favorite bands at the time, before their release of *Meteora.* They were just getting into the promotional stage when the leak occurred. I had been slated by *YouthCulture* magazine (now *Verve Girl* somehow) to interview the band.

It was a dream come true. I would be able to ask the band about all the secrecy that occurred during production of the disc. I would be able to talk about the amalgamation of genres that they so blissfully created and embraced.

They were so freaked by the leaked tracks that they canceled the interview and most of their Canadian stops. The magazine got them to concede to having a representative from Warner Music Group come by my apartment and let me listen to three tracks while the rep watched and then removed the CD, taking it back to the safety of the Warner building. They were even going to send a bodyguard along with the rep, but she was a nice, quiet woman who managed to talk the higher-ups into deeming it unnecessary.

Of course I had only a couple of hours' notice, so I madly tidied the place and popped across the street to get some fresh pastries and milk for her impending visit. The Nice Woman from Warner Music Group showed up, we had the requisite small talk in the living room, I handed her a cup of hot tea, petit fours, the television remote, and a lapful of magazines, and in return she handed me the coveted CD, though you wouldn't know to look at it. It looked like your average blank CD, not something that had years of work and sweat on it.

I went into my bedroom and played it on an old boom box and crazily scratched out notes in an old coil notebook that had a label that said, "Japan" on the cover (I was trying to learn Japanese at the time). I wrote down my first impressions and thoughts, though I was nervous — sometimes songs take two or three listens to really get into your bloodstream. But it was all the time I was granted, so I did the best I could in the few minutes I had with the three or four new tracks.

I went back into the living room and spent about an hour talking with the Nice Woman from Warner. We talked mostly about music, but also about restaurants in the neighborhood, what high schools we went to, and the other small things you discuss with someone you just met.

She left and I spent the rest of the night thinking about Linkin Park and whether they had overreacted. My first reaction was hell yeah, but I then thought, "What if my book had been taken and leaked onto the Net. Would I be upset?"

Hell yeah.

mr. telephone man

I WAS EXCITED to be interviewing Mr. Music Star Anomaly, even though it would be over the phone and not in person. He was one of those artists who, despite being a complete individual, had found success in the mainstream. This was during the promotion of his first album and I truly loved it. The songs went from a trip-hoppy diatribe on living in the smog-filled city to a melodic yet melancholic lullaby to the woman who bore his child.

The interviews I had read with him had thus far been boring, a straight Q & A format, filled with questions about his upbringing and his musical influences.

Yawn.

Like most interviews that I had done up until that point, the editors didn't want creative input or an interesting profile. They wanted me to lob the easy questions, the same questions that the person had been asked 100 times before, over and over, probably ten times in the same afternoon. It gets to the point where, with some celebrities, I know the most intimate information about them, only because everyone including Barbara Walters has asked them about their sexual preference, or what it was like to work with Steven Spielberg on his last film.

I saw this as an opportunity to really delve into his creative soul, to pull away the mask that he had to put on each time he spoke to the media. I wanted to get under his skin and come away with the real person behind the rapper/storyteller.

Luckily, I had an editor who agreed that Q & A's had been done to death and if the magazine was going to branch out into a new style of interview, this was the perfect place to start.

My old tape recorder was just that — old. Old and unreliable. So off to Staples I went and found a very good, mid-price-range Sony that included auto-reverse. (While this was not before digital recorders, they were still relatively new and very expensive. Not like now.) I was thrilled. I felt like the professional journalist I had been calling myself. I imagined this interview leading to someone at the *Village Voice* somehow coming across it, and contacting me through my editor to say that they wanted me to come and work for them. I thought about the movie *Almost Famous*, and how easily I could be William Miller, all of sudden in Ben Fong-Torres's office, discoursing on the perils of both Prince and Lenny Kravitz's last albums. I knew I was getting carried away, but I also believed that dreams come true, and perhaps this was just the first step to a career profiling interesting artists, writers, and musicians.

I spent two days researching and preparing questions. I felt more ready for this than for my final exams back in high school.

On the morning of the interview, my editor phoned to say that the call was delayed by two hours, the hotel's telephone system had ceased to work for the last couple of hours due to a city-wide blackout, and that New York was, well, a complete mess. So, call him at 8 P.M. and it should be back up by then.

I had been preparing for so long that to sit around the apartment for two hours was too much for my adrenaline-filled body and mind to stand. Two hours was barely long enough to watch a movie, so I placed my recorder next to the phone, along with my spiral-bound notepad filled with questions, two Bic pens, and extra batteries, and cassette. I grabbed my jacket and headed out onto the busy street.

Toronto's Mount Pleasant is a major street, but not busy enough to keep me up at night with club music like Queen West. As soon as I hit the pavement, there was that after-work rush that filled the streets. Men in navy suits carrying baguettes and cooked roast chickens rushed along the sidewalk next to moms trying to wrangle their tiny ones back into the stroller so that "we can get home and get dinner started, because Daddy is on his way home, and don't you want to see Daddy?"

I walked up to Yonge and Eglinton, and browsed the books and magazines at the used bookstore. I kept a close watch on the time and decided that taking the bus back would ensure that I was in the apartment with plenty of time to spare before making the call. I picked up two music magazines and caught the Mount Pleasant 64 with forty minutes until PCT — phone call time.

It took ten minutes to get back to the apartment. I put my jacket away and went into my bedroom to go over my questions. I connected my new recorder, tested it, and turned up the volume as high as it would go. I didn't want to take a chance on not being able to hear him over the phone lines.

I made the call at 7:59 P.M. Would he pick up the phone himself, or would it be an assistant, or maybe a bodyguard?

After the third ring, a warm, breathy, "Hello" traveled through the fiber-optic cables and hit me like a pack of Rottweilers hits steak.

I was actually talking on the phone with a famous rapper. My heart was thudding against my chest and my ears were filled with air that was as heavy as lead. All of a sudden, I couldn't hear.

"Uh, hello," I said. I managed to talk through my ear trauma. After introducing myself and saying how much I liked the album, I began the interview. Forty-five minutes later, I hung up. I was still a little shaky, but knew that I had hit gold. He had been warm and forthcoming, like an old friend catching me up on what he'd been doing since we'd last talked.

I pressed stop on the recorder, stood, and stretched my arms above my head. I was so elated, but how to celebrate? Perhaps some sushi from across the street? That would be *perfect*. I grabbed my coat from the hall closet once again and as my hand grasped the doorknob, I thought, I'll just listen to a smidge of the interview before heading out. Just to hear his voice again.

With my coat draped over my arm, I rewound the tape while mentally viewing Oishi Sushi's menu — would I have the seafood udon or avocado maki hand roll?

Click. The tape stopped and I decided on the restaurant's famous hand roll.

I pressed play.

Hiss. Hiss. Hissssssssssss.

No voices. Not his, not mine, just loud hisses.

Like an abandoned telephone call with no one on either end.

first i look at the purse

ONE OF THE THINGS that I started doing while at home was blogging. I kept a blog detailing my thoughts about the writing life, and once I had designed a food magazine online, I started a blog there too.

But those were merely thoughts, event updates, etc. I wanted something with *juice*.

I had been working for a trendspotting site for a while and really enjoyed the work. All of my life I have sought out new products, fascinated by what folks were coming up with. I had only been contributing for two or three months when the editors changed. All of a sudden my ideas weren't being accepted — despite the Mecca of trendspotting sites, *Daily Candy*, running the same idea the next day or a week later. I stopped offering up my ideas, and they stopped e-mailing me about their meetings. No hard feelings on my part. I just wanted to share my ideas with *someone*.

So I started The Knack (http://gottheknack.blogspot.com), a blog where I'd post notes on products I'd found and what they were like after I'd tried them. I enjoyed it and it gave me a great break from all the heavy research-based articles that I'm always working on. I queried companies that weren't getting coverage by mainstream media and after four months, slowly, I started receiving samples to write about.

I was the editor of my own beauty magazine essentially, only covering products that I wanted to, leaving all of the big names out of it. I had started looking for alternatives because magazines at the time only ever featured L'Oréal, Maybelline, and Guerlain. Same went for fashion and home products. How many times did I have to read about the Mr. Clean Magic Eraser? There had to be more than this available.

So I went in search of products that interested me and I thought would be of interest to others. I wanted to cover natural products that weren't making the pages of *Vogue* magazine and so started contacting small companies to try to write about their soaps, cleansers, and cosmetics to see if their claims were true.

According to an article in *Details*, "in a year of daily makeup applications," we absorb "4.375 pounds of chemicals through our skin." I needed to find out how many different companies were going to let me absorb their chemicals through mine.

It started very slowly, but suddenly I was discovering there was a huge world of products behind the main ones we see in the magazines. As our apartment began to look like a department store, I was changing my face creams and cleansing routines every six days in order to cover all the products.

What is interesting is that I am not able just to see what's happening right now, but what's to come. It's about looking at products, not just trends, and seeing what products work, what *lasts*. Who cares if it's "in" if it sucks or breaks after two days of use? The other part of The Knack that I enjoy is that personal recommendations have become more powerful than anything that I or anyone else writes about. It's word of mouth and authenticity, not just press releases and what magazines are telling you is hot in Milan or Paris.

Companies have to work really hard to keep you coming back,

and some aren't doing a very good job. Louis Vuitton has always been a rich person's bag, but when pretty good knockoffs hit the streets (Fucci, Mock Jacobs, etc.), everyone could afford them. Then the idol worship retreated like sales from *Dance 'Til Dawn* (a lovely classic film from 1988 starring — get ready for it — Christina Applegate, Alyssa Milano, Tracey Gold, Tempestt Bledsoe, and Matthew Perry!) and only returned when Marc Jacobs remade them into cool street-ware accessories with his metallic swaths over the stuffy old pattern. But now they've got ads starring Gorbachev staring out of a limo as it passes what remains of the Berlin Wall. Tsk tsk, LVMH. This is no way to get the Soulja Boy crowd wanting your arm-candy.

While there's still successful viral marketing (think *waay* back to Busta Rhymes' "Pass the Courvoisier"), it's neat to see how the online influences are changing our way of viewing products, our purchasing habits, and things like our musical choices. I mean, if you ever use YouTube to watch music videos, you'll see how wrapped up you can get in the artist's other work — or even someone else doing their songs. I mean, have you seen the propensity of singers sitting on a bed, strumming a guitar, doing a heartfelt rendition of "Umbrella," "LoveStoned," or "Wonderwall"?

There is a phenomenon that Jung called "a significant coincidence," which is when "two people have detected a phenomenon of synchrony that releases an unsuspected connection between man, time, and space." And though it is awfully simplified here, I believe that this is truly the way that reviews and recommendations are going — online, interactive, and even live.

I am certainly late to the blogging game, but in some respects, I'm just in time. But trying to stay ahead means constantly updating your idea of what's hot and in turn, that means you're going to need somewhere to put all of this stuff.

Speaking of which, appliances have not only become completely ridiculous and suitable for only one job (Double-Deck Pizza Oven, Margaritaville Frozen Drink Maker, Zarafina Tea Maker, to name just a few), but they are so big, you'd have to live in a house with a kitchen the size of Guantánamo. We don't even have a toaster or blender because of how little storage and counter space we have. I don't think we'll be giving up our dishwashing rack for a behemoth daiquiri maker, or panini machine (like you'd use it more than once anyway), or the chocolate fountain (what are we — a banquet hall?), thank you very much.

One thing I didn't count on were what comes with all the products. For example, getting the new Palm Treo is great. Having the same phone number traveling from journalist to journalist ain't. Late, late, late last Saturday night or early Sunday morning (3:43 A.M.), the Treo rang loudly and scared the hell of me. My heart felt like it was going to push outta my chest. Turns out Roger was looking for Chuck and he should call him back. Same thing last night, except it was 4:28 A.M., it was a different number, and they didn't leave a message.

Who had the phone before me? Do they work at a 24-hour Home Depot? Are they oncologists who work through the night and are trying to get a hold of patients? Or are they security for some after-hours clubs and called to hook up after their shifts to either get blow or maybe just some breakfast at Fran's?

One of the most unexpected joys of The Knack is that I am constantly amazed by the products, how something I originally suspected of being pretty good turns out to be one of the best things I've ever come across (especially the face creams that make me look younger or the lotions that give me an instant tan or remove cellulite successfully!), or how something completely wins me over like a Pod Coffee machine that I had previously concluded gave inferior coffee and was made for lazy folks.

But then there are the insane items that leave you wondering what someone was thinking of, like the Mohawk hat (exactly what you imagine it to be); the T-shirt clock (um . . . exactly what you imagine it to be); the USB drumming snowman; the albino bowler action figure; death-row bubble-gum cigarettes; pickle juice sport drink.

Life is crazy enough without drumming snowmen and sport pickle juice, thank you.

boots of
spanish leather

A PEAR PLUMP from poaching in vodka and covered in hardened milk chocolate sits snug in the bottom of a martini glass, covered and entwined in real ivy vines. A teeny little card attached by a fine string announces a media event next week.

It's quite the invitation. And it's pretty par for the course. Media and PR people can be pretty insane, and if they think you'll write about their product, they'll send you stuff like this.

I look at Scott. "What the hell are we going to do with it?"

"Eat it, I guess?" he shrugs.

About four months after I started blogging about neat products and services that weren't being heavily featured in the magazines I was reading, I started receiving a couple packages a week. By February, I was getting multiple packages a day. As of about a year ago, I started receiving so much that I thought we might have to move. I began calling my neighbors nightly, asking them to *please* come by and take some vodka, potato chips, candles, and tea. Some companies were sending me a case of something so that I could try out every flavor, size, or scent.

It got to the point where I had piles of boxes teetering behind our bedroom door and was constantly rearranging them. Currently the linen trunk at the foot of our bed houses some of the products, along with spillover still left behind the door (the bigger stuff that won't fit in the trunk). There is more where a shelf of CDs used to be, and some food items and kitchen gadgets are out there in the kitchen awaiting trial.

I went to Chinatown and got a narrow little Japanese pantry shelf to hold all of it behind our bedroom door. It's supposed to hold all of your cans and soy sauce bottles, but right now mine's towering with chocolate anti-cellulite cream from Greece, socks made out of corn, all-natural toothpaste from India, a box that transmits your

products lurking behind the door

- Chocolate anti-cellulite cream
- Anti-wrinkle strips that you adhere to your forehead
- A USB hub that is also a fridge (large enough to hold one can)
- Three huuuuge bottles of high-end, sipping tequila
- Candles in the shapes of frogs, owls, seashells, and acorns
- $395 face cream — one of the most expensive on the market
- Sumptuous leather journals from Italy
- Chocolates filled with spicy caramel, chai, burnt sugar, and other unusual flavors
- Back support pillow
- A case of multi-flavored brownies
- Terrycloth flip-flops that fold into a little pouch
- Inhalers that you sniff to suppress your appetite, ease stress, etc.
- Tea like you wouldn't believe
- Organic tampons
- The coolest speakers for your laptop
- Vodka — so much vodka — pear vodka, vodka from the Hawaiian ocean floor, etc.
- Seaweed for making sushi
- Gorgeous sterling silver lightning-bolt necklace
- iPod wireless transmitter
- Gourmet sodas
- Ten see-through watches (and an invoice for $1,000 if I don't return them in good condition)
- Board game that requires you to ask your partner a very personal question
- Stainless steel plant pots

- A keg of micro-brewed root beer
- Reed diffusers that smell like holiday baking
- Lotions, creams, gels — anti-wrinkle, anti-sun
- Tetra-Pak wines
- Social etiquette cards
- World music CDs
- Handmade stationery out of wallpaper, vintage children's books, and letterpressed the ol'-fashioned way
- A case of natural cleaning products that smell like fresh flowers
- The world's thinnest wallet
- Indian cotton yoga pants
- Ziplock bags with skulls and marijuana plants on them
- A full-on vacuum that went around to all of my neighbors for a whirl and scared the bejesus outta the cat
- The world's first magnetized wallpaper
- Jewelry made out of various computer parts
- Perfumes that smell like NECCO wafers, cake icing, crayons, soap, and eggnog
- Soft, plush toys that look like vegetables (for babies)
- Foundation that you spray on
- A smartphone! Wheee!
- A plug that saves you from ripping your ears out when the cord of your iPod gets snagged
- Soaps of every kind — dead sea, shea butter, lavender, olive oil. You name it, I've got it
- Hot sauces — everything from mild mists to wild burning sensations
- Toothbrushes — ultra-sonic, ultra-bristled, recycled, electronic

television to your company via the Internet, a smartphone with a kick-ass camera and keypad, a leather briefcase in burnt umbra that I can't stop touching, shampoos just for the ladies and enough creams and lotions to cover the whole cast of *The Sopranos*. Both sides: New York *and* Jersey.

Now, after doing this for so long, the neighbors won't even come when I tell 'em what I've got. They got so used to the chips and lotions, shampoos, and USB devices that it's old hat. So now I pile stuff in the corner of the living room in various bags and boxes to take for when I see my mom and for friends who I know would like specific things. I try to set aside fun stuff like makeup, jewelry, and clothing for my friend Allison in New York. She's an actor and I always try to contribute to her wardrobe. My friend Camille has been meeting with agents this week, so her bag includes jewelry, makeup, and some lovely perfumes. Recently, I've given away purses, bamboo clothing, and handmade teas from the Himalayas to friends and colleagues.

When I read that, I can't believe people aren't banging on my door to see if stuff has arrived yet. It's the same with restaurateurs and chefs — you'd think they'd be dying to talk to me.

Not so.

I have cases of fresh Fair Trade Certified, organic, whole-bean coffee from the Galápagos Islands, Venezuela, and, I think, the rainforest. Then there's the most accurate watch in the world, a watch that helps you to make decisions, and one that makes suggestions. And did I mention the bottles and bottles of perfumes[8], creams, lotions, and shampoos that I e-mail everyone about? No one comes by and thus I am left with bottles and jars crammed into the bathroom cabinet, on the kitchen table, and even sometimes on my desktop. I'm thinking I need to get a storage unit or at least a large Rubbermaid container for the whole damn lot. It's a wonder Scott, Cosmo, and I can get around here at all.

Everyone tells me what a great job I have — getting stuff to try to then write about. And it is. But it's a heckuva lot of work. I not only have to try everything (you should see the rotations I have us on for coffees, shampoos, grilling sauces, face creams), but I have to read all of the press kits before I write about them. It actually takes quite a bit of time, not to mention having to inventory and keep track of everything. Oh, and don't forget the time researching new products and contacting the companies about them. Then the numerous phone calls and follow-up e-mails that I entertain both from the companies themselves and from their PR people. I have to let them know when the items arrive, when it will be posted, and then e-mail them the day of posting. Over and over again.

---

[8] There are so many celebrity perfumes. Do you really want to smell like Jessica Simpson, Britney Spears, J. Lo, P. Diddy, Usher, Beyoncé, and Celine Dion? And that's just the *musicians*. Other celebrities include Donald Trump, Paris Hilton, Kimora Lee Simmons, Mary-Kate and Ashley Olsen, the Orange County Choppers cast of *American Chopper*, Maria Sharapova, Derek Jeter, and — I am totally not kidding — Alan Cumming. Doesn't it leave you longing for the Jean Naté days?

There's the up and down the stairs with UPS, FedEx, Purolator, and the smaller couriers. Then there's the unpacking of boxes, Styrofoam packing peanuts falling out *everywhere*, and having to store and organize it all. The products over here, the info that came with it over there. Then I have to take all of the packaging downstairs to the recycling bin. This ain't no five-minute thing. One day I swear I'm going to be able to afford an assistant to help me with all of this . . .

In the meantime, you can find me lathering, sipping, chewing, running, digesting, peeling, gulping, soaping, scraping, testing, rinsing, listening, and soaking.

And then writing about it.

hangin' tough

YOU'D THINK BLOGGING would be easier than other writing.

Usually blog posts are shorter than magazine columns and articles, so you'd think that they at least take less time.

Not always.

In fact, when you consider the research and writing that can go into a post, combined with getting suitable accompanying illustrations, then hyperlinking your way through the graphs . . . well, as you can imagine it can take just as long as something that's going to print.

I really want my posts to read like my magazine writing, yet even more intimate, more revealing, more like your best friend telling you about something truthfully, excitedly. Yet, for a lot of folks, blogs just don't cut it. They aren't as *serious* as articles. And I can see that. I mean, there are lots of blogs that are just about people, their friends, and their dating habits. But as we've seen in the 2008 election, the events after 9/11, and Katrina, blogs do offer insights from around the world: they can move you to change, to action.

And a lot of us bloggers don't get paid. I'm spending hours a day writing for The Knack that I don't get paid for. Is it worth it? I think so, because I think I'm filling a niche that is missing from many magazines. And yes, I'd looooove to be paid for it or to make money from it, but I haven't figured out how to straddle the creative with the commercial yet.

I could spend all day doing the blog — writing, promoting, putting up ads, becoming an affiliate, holding contests and draws, and getting an avatar of me with shopping bags and pointy high-heeled boots. But I am a journalist first. As much fun as it is blogging about the latest in jewelry and youth serums, I still want to write engaging lengthy articles for magazines and newspapers about stuff that's not on the blog.

It's weird that I have to keep the two very separate. The editors I write for don't count my blog writing as experience at all — it's the articles and features I've done that get me the work. And yet, magazines are now asking me to blog for them. Huh. It's okay for me to do it for a magazine, but to do it on my own lumps me into the same category as Keri, the nineteen-year-old blogger who writes exclusively about shoes, boys, and shopping (and gets ten times the hits that I do).

The perception remains that it's just some online blithering diary and I'm not actually doing any *real* writing. So why do it when I'm spending all of this time thinking of new topics and not getting paid for it instead of doing the same for magazine work? Why sweat all of the self-marketing to try to get people to come to the site? Why deal with frenzied PR agencies, company CEOs, and the like who don't think that you're good enough, big enough, or influential enough?

Because I am all about the here and now — I no longer read fiction before 1970 and I immerse myself in the latest gadgets, materials, and music. I know that there is something to this, something that has caught the crowd's attention and that it's not just a fad. It's a part of the fabric of news and journalism, and the world we live in. I just haven't figured out how to go from small-known blogger to drawing in the big numbers.

But it can be done. There are a ton of blogs that became insanely popular and then became best-selling books — Julie Powell's *Julie and Julia: 365 Days, 524 Recipes, 1 Tiny Apartment Kitchen*, or *Chocolate and Zucchini: Daily Adventures in a Parisian Kitchen* by Clotilde Dusoulier, or the second book by Gina Trapani, *Upgrade Your Life: The Lifehacker Guide to Working Smarter, Faster, Better*, to name just a few.

It's not that I want to become famous for The Knack or anything else I blog for, but I do believe that it is a kind of communication that is unique and of the moment. It transcends paper, reaches out of the computer screen, and holds you captive.

I love the freedoms that come with writing at length about the thickness of a fabric, the true color of a pottery mug, or the weight of the cardstock handmade letterpress cards, but I hate that it doesn't count as my work.

And trust me, it's work.

I think because it's a *blog* and not a website, people perceive it as being *fun all the time!* GIGGLES AND LAUGHS AND SO EASY TO DO! ANYONE CAN DO IT!

But I'm here to tell you it's as hard as it is fun. Just like most other writing.

hamburger lady

I SHOULD HAVE known that part of my life would be about food. Even as a young girl I had a strange fascination with groceries.

My sweet, sweet mom would let me take all the cans and boxes of various beans, oats, and flours out of the cupboards and set them at one end of the Early Canadian dining room table. I would set up my little cash register at the other end and I'd start ringing in the groceries. I loved it and could do it for hours.

I'm not sure why, but cash registers, adding machines, and type-writers have always had an allure for me. We used to go to country antique fairs where I would spend my allowance on whatever bulky, dusty, rusty adding machine I could find. I would come home so excited and cha-ching the night away.

Clearly I should have been put on some kind of heavy medication.

But the cash register fascination lasted a long time. I worked at a neighborhood fine food store in my late teens and while I enjoyed the stimulation of learning the different areas — bakery, deli, meat department, and produce — I loooved being on cash. I think because it was so orderly — the items went into the bag, a total was shown, and change was given. There was little room for error.

I wonder if my mom ever worried that I would end up being a cashier for the rest of my life? I know as a moody teen, it had crossed my mind. That, or a real-estate agent.

Then there was another long period where I would beg my mom for those "Guest Checks" pads that waitresses would use to take your order (clearly my paper worship began early too). I think I liked this because we didn't really eat out. On vacations, we'd stop in truck stops, roadside diners, and friendly neighborhood joints that often had homemade soups and burgers.

At home, Mom cooked delicious and healthy food (I love turnip, Brussels sprouts, and liver and onions because of her — if that's not a testimonial, I don't know what is), but I do remember the occasional outing, like going to the Red Lobster when it opened up. I was wowed by how fancy it was — all the red booths, the salad that came to the table in big bowls accompanied by scones, and oodles of options. As a kid, I remember that mostly our outings were to the Burger Shack, a little place just on the other side of Eglinton Park, owned by a Greek family. They made wonderfully juicy, flame-broiled homemade burgers and thick-cut fries with smooth, beefy gravy (it's still there, but I don't know who owns it now). My dad and I and our beautiful half-Lab, half-sheepdog Bogie (picture a black Chewbacca) would walk through the park, cross at the lights, and head into the steamy warmth of the Shack.

We would get three burgers and fries with gravy. I loved watching them being made and the toppings were put on just like at Harvey's — I'd peek through the glass and point at the big stainless steel bowls of condiments. I always got extra pickles and for some reason at the Shack I always had the barbecue sauce, though I think that was the first and only place I'd ever had it.

They'd wrap the burgers in waxed paper and put the cardboard containers of fries and gravy in a paper bag, my dad would pay, then slip the bag into the front of his navy peacoat, put up the collar, light his pipe, and we'd head home.

Our house was only about ten minutes through the park and the whole time both Bogie and I could smell the food. Bogie would jump and nuzzle my dad's coat and I too could think of nothing else.

There was something awfully romantic in everything still being warm when we got home and eating this fun and exotic food with my parents. It was such a treat that I savored every moment. And every bite.

So the whole "Guest Check" thing kind of makes sense, but my poor parents — for months, every time they ate, I was ringing up their food on the cash register or adding up their bill as they finished: "Okay, Larry, you had two coffees, a soup, and a sandwich, and Mom, you had two teas, and soup, and a sandwich. Now normally I would give you the daily special price, but it's after four, so I'm going to have to add it up individually."

Charging my parents for food they bought for all of us. What a weird little bird I was.

Am.

Whatever.

I wasn't one of those girls who ended up waitressing very long. I did a little bit at a cappuccino bar and at a couple of other places, but not more than a couple of weeks. I was good at it, but it didn't interest me. I think because it was about being around people, but you couldn't really talk to them or learn about them. How was I supposed to ask questions about them when they're nattering on to their friend about the horrific kitchen renovation that was resulting in her husband sleeping in the den?

My dad and I still eat in diners and small family-run places where they have a cheap breakfast special and the coffee cups are low, wide, come on a saucer, and with as many refills as your stomach can handle. My mom and I try new foods together at places around the city, but if there's liver and onions on the menu, we giggle with delight. We can't stop ourselves.

An order of two, please.

(you gotta) fight for your right (to eat well)

IN AUGUST 2007, Scott Joseph, restaurant critic for the *Orlando Sentinel*, gave his Bill of [Diners'] Rights: "It occurred to me there is no diners' bill of rights, and one is sorely needed. So, if I were a restaurant owner, these are the things you could expect from my place of business. Feel free to share this list with the restaurateur of your choice." His list included no one asking him if he's "still working on that," not waiting longer than thirty minutes for an appetizer, and the check not being delivered to the table until requested.

I'd like to add my own:

- When you first arrive at the table, do not say, "Can I take your drink orders?" While we may indeed be thirsty, this makes it very difficult for us to order our food at this time and sometimes we're really hungry, or we know that your restaurant is especially slow to get dishes out so we want to tell you what we want right away. Maybe, "What can I get you to eat and drink?" leaves us a little more room.

- Please refill my water glass even if it is half-full. I may drink it quickly right after this next bite, and then you won't be 'round for another fifteen minutes (at least) and if I'm eating something spicy and don't have any water, it's coming out of your tip.

- Please, please, please print out your specials and enclose them in our menu or put them up on a board so that we can peruse everything at once and make a satisfying choice. It is so frustrating to pore over a menu for ten minutes, brows scrunched, stomachs growling, and flipping between the line-caught ling, slow-roasted wagyu beef, or the spaghetti pie and then you appear and list off a whole bunch of specials, some of which intrigue, but we quickly forget each one that precedes the next, how much it cost, and what came with it.

- Please do not use a script font that reeks of Beethoven symphonies and ye olde days. I don't want to have to try to decipher whether you're offering filet of sole or pan-fried steak. I also don't want to have to move the menu away at arm's length like I'm June Allyson.

- If you are the type of restaurant that is going to list the ingredients of your salad or entrée, do not bring to the table a dish that has cheese, or nuts, or red peppers on it when it was not listed. You went to the trouble of giving out the list, so why leave anything off? Chances are, I'm not going to want it now, or I'm allergic to the one thing you left off.

- If you are a small little business, with just a counter at the front and a few tables at the back, do us both a favor and get a cordless phone to conduct your business — and explain when payment will be sent — in the back.

Of course, it's not always the establishment's fault if we thought our rights were trampled on. Recently an editor's letter ranted about being asked, "How is everything?" and while he wanted to tell them what was wrong with the meal, he also didn't want to get into a whole uncomfortable argument and simply wanted to finish his meal

Rare duck and quinoa — and this is just the beginning.

without interruption or complication. There are many restaurants that won't do anything even if you say something. But it's up to the diners to be more honest too. A chef recently told me that he went to a friend's restaurant but didn't tell her he was there. She was clearly having an off night — he had two bites of his meal and simply didn't want it. The server kept asking him if he'd like something else and he didn't. He also didn't want to finish the dish in front of him. He pleaded with the server not to say anything to the chef, and instead explained that he just wasn't feeling well and he wasn't upset in the least. The chef came out to see what was wrong and he continued with his story of coming down with something. She ended up suspicious; he ended up hungry.

There's got to be a way we can be honest without being hurtful. After all, that's the only way we're going to make things better. And enjoy our meal.

memphis soul stew

MANY PEOPLE my age (mid-thirties) and older grew up with food that today must seem so odd and antiquated, mostly for its processed lack of nutrition — pork chops smothered in Campbell's cream of mushroom soup; liver and onions; Tahiti Treat; Rice-a-Roni; meatloaf made with Lipton's French onion soup mix and topped with ketchup; iceberg lettuce salads with Thousand Island, French, or Catalina dressing; salmon cakes; Hamburger Helper; tuna casserole; Country Time Lemonade; Jell-O; and ice cream cakes from Baskin Robbins.

Now people are becoming educated and interested in healthy and local foods, courtesy of the Food Network, celebrity chefs, and a plethora of cookbooks being published. Eating locally and organically has brought about a real change in the way we approach the plate. People are much more adventurous, willing to try on new dishes and ingredients. It is perhaps the best time to be reviewing restaurants.

Though I am curvy and could stand to lose ten pounds, it is not the era of cream and butter sauces, thick fatty cuts of meat, and desserts mostly composed of whipping cream, chocolate, butter, and sugar. I still have to consume a lot of calories in a meal — what most people consume in a day — but I also have the luxury of having lean new foods like ostrich, whole wheat pasta, raw fish, and fresh, barely-cooked vegetables.

But there are some things that remain the same.

In interviewing many chefs, only two have been women. And people continue to like red meat, French fries, shrimp, wings, duck, sushi, pizza, and homemade desserts. And as they say, there is no accounting for taste: Allen Iverson likes his chicken fingers with Thousand Island dressing, Jay Leno won't eat or drink any hot liquids, and my favorite breakfast is what you would probably only consider as suitable for dinner. M. F. K. Fisher wrote that "almost every person has something secret he likes to eat." And every year on the list of "guilty pleasures" published by known chefs and foodies, KFC, McDonald's, Kraft Dinner, and frozen desserts from the supermarket are mentioned the most.

We all have those things that make us excited despite their lack of making it on the "it" lists of the year.

Or decade.

And that's what connects us. Food and our history with it.

too much pork
for just one fork

"Forty-two percent of respondents who have dined out in the past year agree or strongly agree with the statement, 'By 3:00 P.M. I usually know if I will be eating a home-prepared dinner that night or purchasing from a restaurant.'"
— Source: R&I, 2007 "New American Diner Study"

AS SOON AS PEOPLE ask what I do and I reply, "restaurant reviewer," the first thing ninety-eight percent of people say is, "Wow, that must be so much fun! You get to try all the new places, eat great food. You are sooo lucky!"

And they are absolutely right on all four counts. It *is* fun and I do get out to the new joints in the city, trying new food. And I *am* sooo lucky. For a girl who used to cater as an excuse to cook for others, combining my love of food and writing is something I had always dreamed of, but never imagined having the opportunity to do myself.

I use to pore over restaurant reviews, fascinated by the vocabulary and the nuance of language. I loved being transported into a steamy Chinese restaurant, with white plastic tablecloths, the air thick with black-bean scent and that bloated feeling that comes with too many small cups of green tea.

But while the idea of eating out all of the time is a romantic one, it is not as carefree as it sounds. For one thing, you have to get dressed to go out. Most nights I don't mind and a lot of nights I look forward to it, but some evenings, I just want to stay in and have a bowl of soup while reading a great book — leave the high heels and swingy dresses behind.

And because I have a '40s mentality, when I go out to eat, I get dressed up. To me, it's a celebration, an occasion that hopefully will be memorable.[9] Most of the time when I go out to eat and review, I wear a dress or skirt. It's old-fashioned I suppose, but I feel professional and dressy, two things that help put me in the mood for the task (and food) at hand.

There is the problem of eating the day of a review. I once tried reviewing one place at lunch and another at dinner. That night, I awoke at 4 A.M. with an intense ache that comes from doing a thousand sit-ups at a time. The problem? The "light" lunch that consisted of foie gras, stuffed lamb chop, scallop salad, and dessert that was followed by a heavy Italian meal that consisted of foie gras, duck, lamb, and venison, never mind the homemade gnocchi (with duck!), antipasto, and three rich and creamy desserts. And that doesn't even include the wine.

After having duck four times that day, along with the tens of other dishes, I vowed to only review one restaurant per day. Otherwise, I would be doing nothing but eating and digesting. And getting fat.

That brings me to one of the most difficult parts of the job. Because it is often a large dinner, not always had right at the dinner hour, I have to plan my other eating carefully around that. I make sure that if I am going out in the evening, I eat lightly throughout the day, often just cereal at breakfast and maybe a salad for lunch.

---

[9] I can remember exact dishes ordered by myself and others since about 1991, but I still have trouble locating Turkmenistan on a map.

Then there is the digesting that goes on afterwards. Often I am eating to my limit. Not always puking full, but trying a whole whack of dishes can fill a girl up in a short amount of time, no matter how little she has of each thing. I'm also eating because I haven't eaten much else that day so I am hungry. Sigh. You have to remember that while eating out four nights a week sounds glamorous, it is not often that I have what I *feel* like eating. I love going out for Thai, Japanese, and Indian, but I have to keep the reader in mind and not just order three appetizers instead of a main. Often I will order something that I might not be in the mood for because it is the restaurant's specialty, or something that is said to wow the crowd. I end up trying a lot of fantastic foods, but I have been at the point where if I have one more lamb shank, I am going to throw up.

Then there is the afterward, the part that — although I've read most of the big restaurant critics' bios — I've never seen mentioned.

Here's a little tour of the after-effects: you are full, bloated, and feeling like a buoy, bobbing on treacherous waters. It's a good thing your skirt has an elastic waistband and Lycra has become your best friend and closest confidante. You have consumed approximately eight different animals in under two hours and the amount of alcohol that is coursing through your veins is reminiscent of the Algonquin Roundtable's entire night's order.

It is only 6:30 P.M. and you have eaten like it is the last meal on the ship. Now you must stagger home and write. This is the last thing that I ever want to do after a restaurant visit. A drunken nap is usually first and foremost on my mind and then something that doesn't involve any heavy lifting. I am usually exhausted afterwards, my body burbling and groaning against its recent intake. The alcohol is something that is a part of the meal more and more often these days, and comes paired with the meal and said courses — meaning, of course, that I can have three or four small glasses of wine during dinner. That is two or three more than I can usually handle. It makes it awfully hard to sit down at my lovely desk and laptop and write anything more than, "Blurhhhhh." Sometimes if I have a coffee, I can work an hour or two later, but it is quite the comedown. It's like that first hour that you get in from the office, especially if it's late at night. The last thing you want to do is anything work-related. You need to relax for a while. This is, after all, human nature and part of working in the big city.

When people go out to eat they do it because they want the total dining experience — selecting what to eat from a range of items, being waited on, having food prepared in a way that's different (and perhaps better) than at home. Being with friends, family, or being surrounded by strangers, there is a magic that comes with dining out.

When I eat out for work, it is enjoyable, but it's work. I'm interviewing the chef, making notes, concentrating on the food's texture, taste, appearance, the room's décor, and the list of items on the menu. Not only am I taking notes the entire time, but I'm actively *listening*. Most chefs I speak to are a sheer delight and it can be exciting to talk food with someone with this much knowledge. But when a chef is going on and on about how famous he is, or how much people love his food, it can be incredibly taxing.

five indian restaurants in eight days

Sometimes I'll eat a lot of the same type of food in one week. In this particular week, it was Indian, and, along with the week that happened to be almost exclusively French restaurants, it has been the hardest of my career — and on my waistline.

Sunday: Restaurant #1
Pappadums
Badami Murgh Tikka (cubed chicken breast marinated in mildly spiced yogurt)
Mushroom, peas and paneer
Chicken Lababdar (broiled pieces of tandoori chicken tikka finished in a cream tomato sauce)
Pulao Rice
Naan

Tuesday: Restaurant #2
Pomegranate Prawns in Banana Leaf
Mewa Kebab (comprised mainly of ground chicken cooked in the tandoor)
Striped Bass Curry
Butter Chicken
Rice
Naan

Thursday: Restaurant #3
Butter Chicken
Patrani Machchi (banana leaf–wrapped halibut with a rich coconut sauce complete with 21 spices)
Basmati Rice
Garlic Naan

Friday: Restaurant #4
(I think I am getting a reprieve
from Indian food for the day,
as it's a Nepalese restaurant,
but just my luck — they
also specialize in Indian)
Yellow Lentil Pappadums
Mixed Vegetable Pakoras
Momo Chicken (Nepali-style
steamed chicken dumpling)
Hariali Tikka ("Green" chicken)
Chicken Tikka Masala
Aloo, Tama and Bodi (pota-
toes, bamboo shoots, and
black-eyed peas cooked
with "mountain spices")
Masala Naan
Rice

Monday: Restaurant #5
Balti Ka Khana Khazana
(a stir-fry dish)
Balti Murgh Kalimirch (pieces
of chicken cooked with fresh
crushed black pepper and
aromatic Baltic gravy)
Machi Na Curry Chawal
(white fish)
Kolmi Na Curry Chawal
(black tiger shrimp in a spicy,
tangy Parsi-style curry)
Methi Roti
Tandoori Roti, garnished
with fenugreek
Pudina Kulcha (a leavened flour
mixed with mint and baked)

I mostly go at odd times of day and night, and sometimes just a few minutes after the doors have opened. I sit alone almost always, which means I sometimes feel like one of those shadowy folks in a bleak Edward Hopper painting. Sometimes as I'm interviewing a chef, he'll have something brought over and then watch me eat it. When I first started out, this made me extremely uncomfortable, but now I don't think about it as I tear into the squab, pieces flying out of its middle, shreds of spinach in my teeth. All in a day's work.

I may be having a lovely meal, but it's not the same as going out with friends. Sometimes it's hard to convince them that it's okay that we go to somewhere I've already been. They don't realize that it's not at all the same. I can go again without being noticed, and experience the restaurant from a pure dining perspective. I love that.

Before reviewing restaurants for a living, Scott and I would spend all of our "extra" money on eating out. It didn't matter whether it was inexpensive Indian or high-end French. We just wanted to experience new things.

Sadly, we don't get to eat out together as much. I am at restaurants in the evenings a lot during the week, but I do bring home some pretty fantastic takeout and all of this good eatin' has really improved my cooking. But the times we do get to go out for dinner, just the two of us? No writing, no cleaning up — just us talking and being together after a busy week? Absolute bliss.

And the best part? I can order whatever the hell I want.

you never met
a motherfucker
quite like me

I'M GOING TO get into a lot of trouble.

I do restaurant reviews the opposite to how the famous ones do it. I never blast a restaurant unless it warrants it. It is like this for me whether I am reviewing a book, CD, or meal. I will certainly point out if something is bad or needs improvement, but I am not ashamed to point out the good stuff.

This makes me unliked by a lot of critics in the city. I am not critical *enough*.

But that's why I call myself a reviewer and not a critic. I want to be honest and fair, not brutal or mean for no reason. I am not disparaging, and I am not about to change. I know there are people who would say I am not a "real" reviewer. But I know there are other people out there who want to know the full scope of what a restaurant offers, and how it holds up against the competition without the expletives and dressing down of chefs and their fare.

While I realize that being anonymous has its merits, I want to know why there can't be another type of restaurant reviewing that's accepted. The kind I do. The kind that lots of people do, not just me. In fact, I have been to media dinners where supposedly "secret" critics dine amongst us — and make sure that their presence and name are known. Not so anonymous, after all. I have chefs tell me all the time about how so-and-so came in and called them over, asking them about this and that, saying who they were.

I am a journalist and so I can be objective, but there is still the air de mystère that comes with the job because no one knows what I'm going to write and only I can say what I had. No one can sway me or buy my good reviews.

One thing I have over some of the other reviewers in the city, the ones who write badly and crudely, is that at least I get it right. I get the ingredients, methods, and histories of the dishes right — because I've done my homework and talked to the chef. This means that no, I am not anonymous.

But I *am* incognito in the fact that I don't work for a daily paper with a readership of a million people. I work for a website where we get hundreds of thousands of hits a day, but I don't have to work within the antiquarian constraints of newspaper critics. That means no one knows who I am anyway. The people the restaurateurs and chefs are after are the few elusive folks from the papers. They think of me as just another staff writer, so contrary to what you may think, I rarely get preferential treatment. Instead, I get talk of increasing customer satisfaction, menu updates, financial targets — it's not about seeing that I get exquisite service, lots of attention, etc. In fact, sometimes I get worse service. Often servers could care less about me so they don't refill my water, and they rarely bother to tell me about the specials. And because restaurant owners and chefs rarely have a free minute, talking to me is not usually at the top of their list (understandably), so I am often left and sometimes even forgotten about at a table. That's why I'm at a restaurant for so long — they're taking phone calls, orders, seeing to other customers. This doesn't happen at every restaurant. Some chefs and owners are just lovely and make me feel very welcome (as they do for *all* of their customers), but for the most part, it's not overflowing champagne glasses with our heads back laughing over piles of ostrich, caviar, and $100 steaks.

So I *can* go into these places and interview the folks, try the food, and write about it objectively.

This is, of course, going to piss off the newspaper critics. But they've got enough troubles of their own — one critic that goes incognito is writing so badly and making so many vital mistakes that I receive the wrath for her from chefs, not only because her reviews get personal, but because she has gotten ingredients and facts wrong. Even her follow-up questions aren't helping. It happens at least at every fifth restaurant I visit. I may not be anonymous, but at least I'm getting my facts straight. But the drama and outrage must sell papers.

A picture of one of the city's best and most well-known critics (who has managed to keep her real identity a secret for the last couple of decades) was posted on a blog. It turns out that chefs across the city have been circulating "secret" pictures of her for years, so clearly she is not as anonymous as she might think she is.

There is this old-fashioned concept of costumes, disguises, and three visits, but when you're working in a city with three thousand restaurants in the downtown core alone and you're one of just a few reviewers, there's no time for that kind of old-school thinking.

Restaurant reviewing is the last bastion of chauvinism. Men mostly go as themselves, but it's the women who have donned the disguises. When the *National Post*'s Jacob Richler and *Toronto Life*'s James Chatto[10] walk into a room of a restaurant where they have interviewed the chef, no one thinks twice about it, but when I mention that I have, people gasp like it's 1932 and I've just told an off-color joke after stealing a crate full of puppies.

---

[10] In the November 2006 issue of *Toronto Life*, resident restaurant critic James Chatto decides to go to work in disguise yet says, "Well, I've been writing about these chefs and their restaurants for nearly twenty years. I've interviewed most of them, spent time with them in their kitchens, found out far more about their work than I ever could by hiding on the other end of the phone. It doesn't stop me from being objective." He goes on about how he goes about trying to make himself inconspicuous, then the accompanying photo is him before the transformation. So just in case you didn't know what he looked like before, you — and all the rest of the kitchens in the city — do now.

In an article from August 2007, a Philadelphia critic was going to be sued by a restaurant over his review and his worry was about his anonymity. Why? Apparently, he too has the notion that full beard and wig is mandatory for reviewing food. An article in Grub Street argued that disguising oneself shouldn't be part of a restaurant reviewer's job description:

> We always found the idea of restaurant critics going out in disguise ludicrous, especially the famous ones, like Ruth Reichl or Craig LaBan, whom everybody knew anyway. That's one reason we are behind the *New York Daily News'* decision to allow Restaurant Girl to dine out without getting made up like an actor from a Tennessee Williams play. (LaBan has appeared in public in full theatrical whiskers, in order to avoid blinding onlookers with his power.)

Despite "Restaurant Girl" coming out with many newsfolk championing the idea of not having to cloak yourself, the public still has the old notion that this is how it's done.

But the article goes on to say:

> The truth is that most restaurant critics of note are recognizable, but it doesn't matter: their reviews tend to be pretty accurate, and even when fawned upon by management, they don't necessarily get soigné treatment from the harried food runners. The problem with most critics of LaBan's stature is not anonymity, but tablecloth fatigue.

Adam Platt, a.k.a. The Gobbler, who is the restaurant critic for *New York Magazine* says in his article "How a Restaurant Critic Avoids Getting Made" that in the bigger restaurants, they hire people just to spot the critics and post their pictures in the back room. He argues that "disguises may work for certain ninja-style stealth experts (like Ruth Reichl), but not for the majority of restaurant critics — and certainly not for the Gobbler, who is balding and big as a house." He adds that even if the restaurateur notices the person walking through the door is a critic though, it's not like they can do anything at the last minute to change how the meal is going to go.

So, it turns out I *can* be objective and a professional journalist all whilst eating a meal in a restaurant. I won't be swayed. While I do get to talk to people behind the scenes, I'm still a food lover at heart. So I'll tell you when something's good or not. My favorable reviews cannot be bought.

Or, apparently, my water glass filled.

cut the curtains

I AM SITTING in a newly minted restaurant. It is only three weeks old, yet due to rave reviews (even from the two critics who rarely give a nod) the restaurant is booked for almost the next month, save a Monday or Tuesday night or so.

It is an hour and a half before opening and though it only houses forty-two seats, it is full of energy, anticipation, and much to do by the eight or so staff members who have already been here for hours prepping. Someone swaths a lemony pine cleaner beneath my bar stool and another swabs the counter with a dry cloth. Ice is thrown into a stainless steel bin with a loud crash, awaiting the cocktails, sodas, and water that will be served tonight. Heavy artisan cutlery is placed carefully on the table, and goldfish bowl–sized wineglasses are adjusted to their proper position.

The phone rings incessantly, people pleading to come in — someone is going to see a movie afterwards and wants a guarantee that they'll be out by 6:45, another wants to know the two closest landmarks and asks them to be repeated. Online reservations pour in amid the ringing phone. On the Open Serve program shown on the computer screen, the reservation schedule keeps blacking out times that are being booked online in real time. That means there's 100 people for tonight and it's not even four o'clock.

The restaurant doesn't open until five.

Two people, who look like they have been in the business a long time, rearrange tables to accommodate five deuces. They do a number of formations until they create something out of the ordinary, a rhombus-type setup. It is one of the first things the owner notices upon his arrival and he immediately asks who did it and then warmly thanks them. The kitchen can be seen through smoky gray glass, so only quick glimpses of bodies and swirls of utensils in motion are visible.

Though I am the only one who will be eating here before opening, the kitchen is in full effect — marinating, soaking, patting, frying. It is a host of movements and technique though it is silent on this side of the hazy glass. Staff members continue to stream in, dressed in head-to-toe inky shades. The ones who have been here for the afternoon are asked to change by the manager. The restaurant opens in half an hour.

At the bar, I eat my four plates and bowls of food with abandon — hearty, creamy dishes that alight from their vessels and settle lightly in my tummy. I quip with the staff as they pour me a crisp glass of white wine that lifts the spicy fare and warms me on this chilly night.

At exactly 5 P.M., I head out the doors onto the street. The sun has begun to fade, and the fall air has me pull my coat closer to my throat. I have all the notes and quotes that I need to write my piece. As the sun slowly sets, reflecting off the windows, I am toasty despite the chill air.

take lots with alcohol

YESTERDAY, I began my day as per usual — shower, dress, sit down to the computer, and write for a while. But at 10 A.M., I was out the door because I had seven bottles of tequila waiting to be tested downtown at 11:30 A.M. I would've written about this last night, but I had four tequilas, two tequila cocktails (doubles!), and a tequila shot that resembled a Bloody Mary with an orange twist.

You wouldn't have wanted to see the results of that on the page.

I was careful today. I watched myself at the event and only imbibed in the tiniest of sips. That, and I'd been at a dinner event the night before where a friend and I had a bottle of wine, so I didn't want to get too crazy. It's really hard to write when you're tipsy. For me, I get tired and just want to lie down — not the kind of mood you want to be in when you've got a 1,500-word article due, or have to try to decipher the notes you took during the chef interview where wine was again involved.

Christ.

I never thought my world would be so booze-soaked. When I

was nineteen, I drank a lot of red wine, Sahara-dry dirty martinis, and a few Black Russians here and there, but by the age of twenty-four, I'd had my fill and would prefer just the occasional glass of wine with dinner. Now here I am in a job where I not only usually have a glass of wine with dinner, but the trend is to pair a wine with each course. You should see me at the end of a seven-course meal.

I recently met the incredible wine columnist Margaret Swaine, who in person does not have a red nose, and is not overweight or sporting bloodshot eyes. She actually is very sprightly. I asked her how she does it and she said she works out "a lot," and drinks a lot of water. Perhaps I should speak with Donna J. Cornett, author of *7 Weeks to Safe Social Drinking*. . . .

I counteract the effects of way too much wine with an espresso or coffee at the end of a meal. It is the only way I can make my way home from the restaurants every night without bandying about the subway station like a three-year-old on a tricycle.

This is not just a once-in-a-while thing. In fact, last month I went to four tastings and today I have two. *In one day.* The first one is at noon (they are all held early in the day) at an incredibly well-known fine dining restaurant downtown. The room is packed. It's not my first sherry tasting, but it is a pretty big deal. All of the critics, columnists, and food pundits are here. There are about eighty of us squeezed around tables of eight that are clinking due to the ten glasses of sherry in front of each person, along with a water glass, wineglass, cutlery, and plates of varying sizes.

It is loud and I am one of three people dressed up. A lot of guys with paunches and beards are dressed in Mark's Work Wearhouse jeans and pleated khakis (one with a bursting black plynyl fanny pack!).

I don't know anyone at my table. There are two dignitaries from Spain who smile and nod at me throughout the whole two-and-a-half-hour ordeal, and the young sommelier of this restaurant. He is the only one to spit his wine into a large champagne bucket that started out at the center of the table and now sits beside him on the floor. Every time he swigs, he picks it up, spits, and places it back on the floor. It's a little like watching *Fast Times at Ridgemont High*. Twice. There's also an older guy on my right who looks like he has been sitting his whole life. He's got that hunched-back, baggy, stretched-out-sweater look that was rampant in the '80s and '90s. In fact, I think some people just came for the free drinks and elite food of the famous chef, who pops his head in near the beginning, which causes people to write furiously in their notebooks or on the cover of the booklet we got to accompany our tasting.

Curiously, the seat next to mine has a black "reserved" sign on it. I assume incorrectly that it is for the man giving us a presentation on the different classifications for sherry, soils and barrels required for the process, and other types of things that "matter" while we are all dying to get our drink on. The ten wide glasses have less than an inch of sherry in them and the colors range from pale amber to thick, syrupy, dark chocolate brown. They are accompanied by various little offerings of duck, cheeses, and a homemade wild honey organic ice cream that seems to wow the crowd.

The presentation has been going on for forty-five minutes now and the room is getting restless. During the whole presentation, servers have been bumping by my chair to get out to the center of the room to gather plates and glasses and drop off the next course. I am in the war zone and I'm going to have the bruises to prove it.

Whoever says restaurant critics and food and wine writers get special treatment doesn't know how much we *don't*. Well, not me, at least. But then I see who does.

A seemingly gruff fellow comes in with a mop of disheveled hair and a black box in hand. He sits to my left. He doesn't say anything, but gets a pen from his battered, out-of-date satchel, and begins flipping through the tasting note booklet to see where we're at.

He makes tiny notes in a surprising round cursive hand when a server suddenly removes his ten glasses of sherry. He passes another server behind him his black box. She asks him how many he'd like. "They're on number four now."

"I'll take six to start," and quickly bows his head to his notes. The server brings him the first six sherries in his own Reidel glasses fresh out of the box and says that she'll bring him the rest as soon as he wants them. (I've *got* to start bringing my own glasses with me. But something tells me a Tim Hortons mug wouldn't yield the same results.)

He takes a large, powerful sniff, a smaller sniff, and then a swish of sherry travels 'round his mouth in a way that to me, sitting next to him, sounds like the roar of the ocean. He swallows with a loud gulp and makes six lines of notes for each glass.

It doesn't take him long to catch up to the fifth one we're on however, and the rest of his glasses are brought out to him, while I can't get anyone to take my old glasses away. There is no room to move and the waitstaff is bumping me around like a pinball in the bonus round. I've got to find out more about this guy.

It turns out he's Michael Vaughan, the *National Post* Weekly Wine and Spirits columnist. He is the one who provides the rating on every single alcohol — wine, spirit, etc. — that comes into the country for a newsletter that he puts out. Every. Single. One.

Ohhh. So *that's* why the glasses, the special treatment, etc.

Of course, I don't have this bio handy at the restaurant, so I introduce myself and offer him some of my notepaper because he's making notes around the photo of the sherry bottle in the program that was supplied. He laughs and says he's used to doing it this way and his assistant has learned to read his scrawl.

We form a minute bond and by the time I'm on sherry number seven, he's nudging me. "Taste this one. Taste the clay. Can you taste clay?" he implores.

Uh, I . . . guess?

"Ha!" he yells. "If it tastes like clay, it means it's off, that something didn't go right in the process."

Huh.

I grab the next glass, praying that the sad little portion of bread and cheese not fit for a mouse that was served will somehow multiply into a big serving of lasagna or chicken or something substantial because we're onto glass eight now — the thick, dark, sweet stuff — and I'm feeling pretty loose.

"Try this one. It tastes like celery."

The man is right, again, but of course he is. He tastes *hundreds a month.*

I tell him I'm going to another tasting after this. He looks at me, completely unimpressed.

"I've got three more," he says, shrugging his shoulders.

Gulp.

"Do you ever just wanna stay home, have a grilled cheese, and watch TV?" I ask hesitantly.

"All the time," he says.

The tasting finally comes to a close and we exchange cards.

I wobble my way to the coat check and catch up with some folks who run this amazing Spanish restaurant down in Kensington. I am swaying, but I'm okay. Just feeling good. Like I could dance all night. But I've got another tasting awaiting me.

guava jelly

"Nineteen percent of respondents spend $50 to $74 in an average week at restaurants and food service establishments."
— Source: R&I, 2006 "Tastes of America"

I AM REALLY, really lucky that I don't have to worry about the cost of the food I eat in restaurants. At least for work.

It can be ridiculously expensive, especially the new ones that I usually end up covering. These aren't $20-for-two sushi restaurants I'm talking about.

Takeout has also gone up in price incredibly.

Remember when your parents used to take you to McDonald's because it was an inexpensive meal out? No longer. In fact, it can cost me the same to get a soup and sandwich at the organic café around the corner as it does for the upsized meal combo.

Crazy.

But some of the things are just too much for me to handle.

Like the $108 pizza that is garnished with 24-karat gold leaf at a café across the street from us. Gimme a break.

But it's not so bad for us in Toronto, or even New York. London, it turns out, is the most expensive city to eat in. And I can see why. Just one example is the recently created world's most expensive sandwich coming in at £85. With ingredients like wagyu beef, fresh lobe foie gras, and black truffle mayonnaise, it's still an awful lot of moola for one little sam.

And this damn craze for all this high-end meat isn't helping. Alberta AAA, Black Angus, Kobe, USDA Prime, and wagyu are currently the rage around the globe and people don't seem at all concerned about spending a whack of cash on what is supposedly quality meat. But be careful. Just because a restaurant says it's wagyu doesn't mean it's the real deal. Make sure to check it out thoroughly before spending a hundred dollars or more. You may just be getting wagyu- or Kobe-*style* meat. They won't put that on the menu of course, but it's not even close to the real thing.

Co-executive chef Grant MacPherson at Wynn Las Vegas said, "The holy trinity of Western luxury cooking is caviar, foie gras, and lobster." That's all fine and good, but it's awfully hard on the waistline. Mine in particular. I am lucky in that most of the food that hits these lips is relatively healthy, but it's not necessarily low in calories. I try to keep trim, but it's a battle. And a lot of my old school heroes — like Jeffrey Steingarten — are not skinny-minnies, so I always have this image in my head of being 300 pounds after a decade of cream-laden pastas, boiled lobsters dripping in butter, and Belgian chocolate terrine.

In the clever book *Lulu Meets God and Doubts Him*, the main character Mia sees a stocky man and thinks, "I can see something appealing about the extra weight he carries as a result of foods like Kobe beef and scrambled eggs with caviar, all washed down with big crystal goblets of expensive wines . . . Dinner with him would be fun."

I worry about that. About all of this eating catching up to me. And while most of my friends are on some kind of diet or regime, I can watch what I eat only at home.

Raw vegetables, lean turkey sandwiches, and homemade vegetable soups all in return for pecan pie, potato salad (mmm — mayonnaise!), brandy butter, duck, hot danish, and fatty crab. It's a pretty sweet deal if you ask me.

eat to the beat

I DIDN'T REALIZE what slow eaters Mom, Dad, and I were until I started dating and ate with others.

My extended family (grandparents, aunts, etc.) all lived extremely far away so I grew up thinking that how Mom, Dad, and I — the whole family (plus big dog) — did things were the norm. And then I'd visit friends with large families and see numerous platters being passed around and grabbed at, how quickly people made their way through the food and plates.

I was always the last one at the table, trying to chew quickly and quietly while the rest of the table politely sat and cleared their throats, trying to mask their impatience. And not only was I a slow eater, but it wasn't until I met Scott that I realized how crumbly and soft my teeth are. Scott has these chompers that are smart, sharp suckers that can make their way through the fattiest cut of meat in a few short minutes.

I, on the other hand, am an entirely different beast.

I was thrilled that I was finally going to be reviewing a steakhouse.

After the umpteenth Italian and Mediterranean dinners I'd consumed in the last three weeks, I was aching for a change. I went in with an empty stomach and was thrilled when the appetizers started coming out hot and fast.

The waiter warned me that the steak I ordered would be the biggest I'd ever have, and patting my hand said in a soft whisper, "It's okay if you don't finish it, hon."

I smiled and said I was sure I'd be fine. People always assume that I can't eat a lot and that I'm a vegetarian. Wrong on both counts. But what I hadn't counted on was this piece of meat.

It was the size of my torso.

But I was so excited not to be having homemade gnocchi or rack of lamb, I dove right in. Big steak be damned, I thought.

I tore into the first bite and it was cooked medium-rare, as I'd ordered (rarely does it come out the way I ask) so as the soft, grassy meat combined with clear bloody juice filled my mouth, I actually closed my eyes to savor the moment. When I opened them, the owner was at my side to ask how it was. The restaurant had been open only six days at this point, so he was eager to get my opinion.

After twenty seconds, he sat down.

I started on bite two, and as he jabbered on about his former restaurant, the method of cooking the beef, and how the cows were raised, I continued chewing this second piece as a small ache begin to form along my jawline.

He kept asking if I was sure I liked it and I continued to nod like I've never nodded before. Like a bobblehead on the dash of a Chevy truck traveling through ski country.

It was closing in on half an hour and I had just begun to chew my third piece.

I was born without wisdom teeth ("No wisdom, that one," my relatives might utter if I lived with them) and had my back molars removed as a young teen.

My mouth is small and crowded with wonky teeth, but none other than my front that are of much use.

Sure I can use my back teeth, and they are crumbly little chiclets that work really hard, but frankly, they aren't up to the task of restaurant dining and reviewing — crisp vegetables that result in loud crunches, crispy pork belly, rubbery calamari that take a lot of hearty chewing and mouth work, and seaweed that requires sharp teeth to tear into and get a clean break.

I get by, but I know that strong teeth would make me a dining fiend.

And suddenly I'd find myself with a couple of extra hours in which to while away the day.

Maybe by ordering a nice fatty Montreal smoked-meat sandwich on rye, some buttery popcorn, and crunchy celery and carrot sticks.

Mmm.

banquet

PEOPLE OFTEN ASSUME that because I review mostly fine-dining restaurants that going somewhere where the entrees are less than $25 is going to disappoint me.

In fact, it's the complete opposite. I love going to rundown places where only the neighborhood folks go and there is no chance of it ending up in *ZAGAT*. The food is often great. And I'm all for dinner for two for twenty bucks. In fact, bring it on. I'm just as happy with a big bowl of homemade soup and great company, or cheap sushi and the newspaper.

As a teenager and young adult, I used to get great joy out of the every three- to five-year trip to the Mandarin, that chain of Chinese buffet restaurants where the food seems to go on for miles. For birthdays and office parties, it was the natural choice, as it cost little more than going somewhere else, and we could all eat as much as we liked. We'd wait only a second beside the koi pond in the entrance to be seated. Despite our large numbers, there was always room for our party.

I'd be able to go and get any number of combinations in whatever amount I wanted. Though I was an avid and good cook, Asian flavors were never quite the same when I made them at home.

It was a poor girl's heaven — and I could get all of the greens I could handle thanks to the hefty salad bar; that was always the truthful draw. If the next day I mentioned my lettuce frenzy at the Big M, friends would chide me for not getting my money's worth — apparently I should have been stuffing myself with crab legs, steaks, and chicken balls. My attention was required elsewhere, I was told time and again.

But it didn't matter. I would get my one and a half plates of hot selections from the center aisle, but it was the coleslaw, chef salads, pickles, and raw vegetables that I was after. When I was seventeen or so, a boyfriend and I went for dinner there. I apparently had such an effect on the staff — they'd never seen someone love raw veggies so much — that they sent me away with a red-and-white egg roll cardboard box full of celery and carrot sticks for the way home.

Fast-forward to almost twenty years later, and the Mandarin is still there — in all its glory — except the koi pond at the entrance is gone. I bet it was all those pennies that people threw in, knowing full well it would erode and then slowly kill the giant goldfish.

buffalo stance

"Grilled/broiled chicken was more likely to be ordered by Millennials (ages twenty-six or younger) and Gen X consumers (ages twenty-seven to forty-one) compared to matures in the past twelve months."
— Source: R&I, 2007 "Tastes of America"

WHILE I GET to eat lovely and exotic foods, they generally don't tend to get too "exotic." New places often do something that's been done before, or isn't so out there that people won't try it. Older places stick to what works for them, and avoid anything trendy and strange.

I do get my share of sweetbreads, a dish made of the pancreas or thymus gland of an animal younger than one year; whole fish ("save me the eyes!"), beef cheek (tongue *and* cheek every once in a while); exotic meats (mostly served raw these days as carpaccios); frog, and other glistening, wobbly sea creatures that would make most of my friends start to heave. It's rare, but sometimes I'll be offered chicken feet (I like 'em golden and crispy over boiled and gray) and recently

I missed out on goat brain — they'd just sold the last one moments before I arrived.

Exotic and wild meats are very much in fashion right now and so throughout the week I can consume a fair amount of bison/buffalo, elk, rabbit, venison, wild boar, Kobe beef, ostrich, pheasant, and squab. We don't get much alligator, antelope, caribou/reindeer, crocodile, llama, musk ox, rattlesnake, yak, or guinea fowl this way, though hopefully that will change in the next year or two.

One of my favorite steakhouses recently started a "Wild Game Night" the first Monday of every month, where they serve many of the usual suspects, but also have kangaroo on the menu — the first time I've seen it on a menu here in the city. (I've had it since at another restaurant that has it on the menu year-round. It is fantastic.) The whole "nose to tail" movement and serving organic meats that are low in fat has made getting these at a restaurant (and at your local grocery store) much easier. And to figure out what to do with it all, *The Whole Beast Cookbook* by Fergus Henderson should offer some guidance.

But there are some things I've yet to have on the job — no chicken lips or dancing shrimp, a dish described by blogger Vehere thusly: "The shrimp are dancing because they are alive. Coated in spices sure to melt your insides, the shrimp are tossed in the spices, and put in a Styrofoam container. The shrimp are then served with glutinous (sticky) rice, or as I had it that night cucumber slices." And surprisingly little haggis (stuffed sheep's stomach or intestine) comes my way. But never say never.

In Japan, there are remote little restaurants that serve exquisite fish that you won't find here. We think we're so exotic ordering eel and mussels, but what about whale skin or whale ovary?

There are still some foods, however, that remain controversial here in the big city. Like horse. I've had horse a number of times and the first time I had it was the best. It was at this little tapas place down on Queen Street and it came to the table hot and crispy — even a little burned at the edges. The meat was tender, salty, and included the tiniest little crisped fat bits. It was quite the heady experience. But if you eat it and (gasp) like it, it might be best to keep the tales of your new favorite dish to yourself. I found this out the hard way.

I was at a party, and by 8 P.M. I had a headache and couldn't believe people in their thirties still acted like this. There was an open bar and it seemed people just couldn't get enough of the stuff. Luckily, I started talking with the wife of a friend and we hit it off. Despite the cackling and stumbling that went on around us, we found a some-what quieter corner and talked about books, writing, and the things that really excite us. I was grateful for the intellectual stimulation amidst the *Animal House* reenactions.

They offered to drive me home (hallelujah!), and as we talked and laughed, I was already starting to feel better. Inevitably, as always, the discussion turned to restaurants and I told them about places I had just been, dishes I had consumed.

Then I told them about the horse.

Not a good idea.

The wife's eyes filled with tears and her mouth quivered as she told me that she *looooved* horses, and they are such warm and intelligent creatures. As we pulled up to my building, I was still floundering to find new ways to apologize and to soothe this poor woman.

Good thing I didn't tell her about the fantastic rabbit I'd had in Yorkville . . . .

pleasure is all mine

"Forty-one percent of [Torontonians] go out to dinner less than once a week."

— Poll results published in *Toronto Life* magazine, April 2006

WHEN I WAS about twelve, my mother was out one night and I decided to cook my dad dinner.

I doubt I'd been at the stove before this, unless it was at my mom's side to "help" her (read: eat the slices of raw turnip. She'd have to peel and slice to whole thing just to get a wee little bit of cooked rutabaga for us for dinner because I couldn't get enough of the raw stuff).

So I rooted around the cupboards and decided I would invent something.

My dad likes softened foods and so canned tuna and tomato paste seemed the perfect concoction and even at twelve, I had a propensity for making a quick meal. (I was making thirty-minute meals from start-to-finish long before Rachel Ray. Even now I can make an entire meal out of condiments. Just ask Scott.) My dad probably ate as much as he could and I do remember him saying, "It's good, pumpkin," which in Pa speak is gratitude beyond belief. But it must have been pretty awful. Just last week though, I was in an Italian restaurant where an appetizer featuring tuna in a heavy tomato sauce was being touted as one of the restaurant's signature dishes. It's not exactly the same, but it shows I was on to something.

I have been actively cooking pretty much every other day since I was fifteen. When people come over for the night, I make a mess of food. So much that it could probably feed us, our company, the neighbors and the Rosicrucian Center down the street. I can't help it. I can't stand the thought of someone not being able to have enough or take enough for fear there will be nothing left. I don't know where this comes from. I'm an only child and I don't remember my mom making Pa and me have leftovers for days like some kids growing up. In fact, I don't remember leftovers much at all.

I know I'm overcompensating, trying to get people to like me by offering not one, but three pasta salads . . . but I'm not the only one.

My friend's mom orders three times the normal amount at restaurants, ensuring that everyone will go home with a sizable doggy bag. Our neighbor downstairs had a few of us over for dinner one night and made about forty burritos — twenty vegetarian, twenty chicken. Funnily enough, the seven of us just about cleaned her out.

I have known for a long time that food is love: the time I made tuna tomato for my dad and he ate it with nary a flinch, the time I burned an omelette at four in the morning for a guy I was seeing and he finished it without scraping one iota of black ash back onto his plate, staring at me all the while, and the way Scott makes me a roast chicken dinner that is perfection every time.

There is love in dem dere bones.

More chicken?

sukiyaki

EVERYONE TALKS about restaurants and dishes being *authentic*, but if you are eating at a Japanese sushi restaurant and the guy working the sushi table is not Japanese or doesn't look comfortable with a knife, you may not be getting the real goods.

Did you know that probably a lot of the fish you're consuming at those fast-food Pan-Asian places was frozen? Your sashimi and nigiri aren't the real deal — at least, not the way the Japanese have them. So stop telling your friends this is how they do it in Japan . . . because they don't.

California rolls were created in *California*. Though they have made their way back to Japan, they are not a part of the real Japanese landscape. That's like saying that the frothy Nescafé powder that debuted in the '90s that you have to stir, stir, and *continue stirring* until your arm falls off is really cappuccino.

I don't think so.

I think part of the problem is there is a large contingent of wealthy business folks who travel a lot, eat out in fine-dining establishments just as much, and use their expense accounts to pay for it all. These are the people who get caught up in the trends, frequenting new restaurants that offer melon foam soup and fried mayonnaise. They deem a place worthy, but whether it actually is or not can be seen by the vicious comments of sites like Chowhound.com and *New York* magazine's Grub Street.

It is hard going up against the mythology of a restaurant — of its looks, its chef, or its clientele. It's like trying to say you don't like Margaret Atwood's stories. Don't even try it.[11]

Restaurant groupies forget the six months of bad reviews and retelling of the chef's ineptness to cook the meat to anything but well-done. Everything has been refracted since Rachel McAdams, Ryan Gosling, and Lauren Conrad were seen eating there. You can't stop the crowd after that. You can only shrug your shoulders and hope that people who really care about food will see through the façade.

That and that your fish will be defrosted properly.

---

[11] I did once, in a magazine for writers. In fact, I got my first hate mail, where someone had torn the article out of the magazine and underlined ninety-five percent of the text and then filled in their comments about my obvious lack of intelligence and school-ing, my wrong, wrong, *wrong* opinions, and my dark future of being nothing, going nowhere, etc.

don't stop believin'

WHEN I FIRST started cooking, catering, and writing about food, I'd get very upset when people would ask me what Canadian cuisine was and I didn't have a definitive answer. Elk and horse were too exotic, salmon and seafood had been claimed by New England and California already, and Canadian back bacon was just something that Americans made fun of us for. Everything else that I could think of was too regional: Quebec has tortière and poutine, Alberta has their beef, and even Ottawa has beaver tails, a flat fried pastry topped with lemon juice, cinnamon, and icing sugar.

Twenty years later, I have just recently discovered the heart of our cuisine.

Although I have not traveled as much as some of my closest friends — Antarctica to photograph penguins, and off to India for six months of adventure — I have seen enough to know that in Canada we are all about seasonal fare, local produce, and offering every available cuisine within a short distance.

Scott and I reside in the Greek area of town, but we have within

Searching for the perfect ingredient . . .

a fifteen- or twenty-minute walk Chinese, Japanese, Italian, Thai, Ethiopian, Vietnamese, Mongolian, French, and Egyptian fare. Canada is multicultural, especially here in the big city. You can get tom yum (Thai lemongrass soup), ma po bean curd (Szechuan minced pork bun with hot bean sauce), aloo chana chat (Indian potatoes and chickpeas with spices), linguine ai frutti di mare (pasta with seafood), and mujadarra (Lebanese rice and lentils topped with fried onions), all without trying too hard or having to go too far.

But according to many new books and cookbooks on the shelves, there actually *is* a Canadian cuisine. *The Canadian Cookbook: History, Folklore and Recipes with a Twist* by Jennifer Ogle has a bunch of options, one of which are little cinnamon pastries that, when literally translated from their French name, are "Nun's farts."

Let's hope the Americans don't find out about that one. We'll never hear the end of it.

potato chips polka

GOING TO WILLIAMSBURG with my parents when I was thirteen was not the most exhilarating summer trip I could think of, but what excited me most was all of the Americana that we would come across. Having gone to Cape Cod for a week's vacation summers before, I knew what the States had to offer. In a nutshell, everything we didn't have in Canada.

So, pulling up to the inn in Williamsburg wasn't as awful as you might think. While my mom went off in search of beeswax candles made by Mennonites and Early American wing chairs in heavy ticking, my dad walked me down the hill from our room to the store lying at the bottom, or, as I like to think of it, Mecca.

The 7-Eleven store shone like a meteor even though the sky was just beginning to turn to dusk. The colors inside the large glass windows were as bright and manufactured as gumballs — shocking aqua, eye-opening magenta, and a yellow that could only be called Tweety.

I opened the door and immediately a chill set over me. Not just due to sheer excitement and awe, but because the store was lined with freezers and fridges around its perimeter, like a wondrous igloo. Except this igloo was stocked floor to ceiling with every salty and sugary confection that space allowed. The air had that metallic taste to it, and my skinny arms quickly covered with goosebumps.

The smell of vinegary floor cleaner lingered as I wandered aisle to aisle. I was fascinated that beer and wine were right next to Coca-Cola and Mountain Dew. And the store was filled with almost nothing that was good for you. In Becker's, our corner store back home, you could still get brown rice and oranges, despite the aisles of popcorn, marshmallows, potato chips and chocolate bars. Speaking of which, this store stocked ones mostly foreign to me. Weird ones like PayDay, Baby Ruth, and 100 Grand. Their orange plastic packaging was thinner and more crinkly than ours back at home. More like the bars my British grandmother would bring when she visited.

After what seemed like hours of me running my hands over brightly colored items, my dad called me over to the potato chip section. This is where it got exciting. They had flavors I had never heard of before — smoky bacon, roast chicken, and fries with gravy. I was in heaven. My dad quickly filled his arms with a couple of large bags and headed over to get us some Dr Pepper. Even more exciting was the Cherry Coke and Black Cherry Pepsi, nothing like the mere non-flavored versions back home. He said we could have a taste test back at the room.

Having grown up with meals that were made out of oats and soy protein, and no pop or treats allowed in the house, I felt like I had won a trip to Disneyland — the one filled with teeth-aching delicacies. I couldn't wait to get back to the room.

We walked up to the cash. By now, my eyes had adjusted to the hospital-white lighting and I wanted to stay here forever. There was another cooler right beside the register that housed Jimmy Dean sausages, Louis Rich bacon, and burger meat in a cylindrical sausage-like casing. Weird. We always bought a pound fresh at Bittner's. I had never seen it packaged before and never like it was already a sausage.

On the counter was every kind of licorice — strips, wheels, pipes, and whips — in a host of colors, like Granny Smith apple green, mauve, tomato red, tobacco black, Barbie pink, and tangerine. It was like my colored pencils pack had transformed into a stringy, plastic, sugary heaven before my eyes.

Above the cash was a host of American cigarettes like Winston, Marlboro, and Merit. I had seen these at the gas stations we had pulled into along the way and I was struck at how colorful they were, like a large billboard compared to our boring Canadian brands of du Maurier, Player's, and Matinée. Neither of my parents smoked (Pa smoked a pipe), but cigarettes were behind every corner store counter, so it was hard not to notice.

My dad paid for everything (two large bags of chips; a small bag of San Francisco Honey Mustard Sourdough pretzels; a Baby Ruth for my mom, whose name is Ruth; a Cherry Coke, Black Cherry Pepsi, and Mountain Dew) and we exited the store.

The heat hit us like a punch in the gut. We wiped our brows, looked at one another, and smiled as we made the climb back toward our hotel. When we got to our room, my dad pulled out a *TV Guide*, something we didn't have at home either, and said that we could watch some American shows or a movie while we tried out our new finds.

This was going to be the best vacation ever.

chocolate rain

"Three-quarters of respondents say that dinner is the meal of choice for trying both new foods and new dishes when dining at a restaurant."
— Source: R&I, 2007 "New American Diner Study"

ONE OF THE interesting facets of being a restaurant reviewer is that trends become immediately apparent. By eating out so much during the week and assessing so many menus, dishes, and ingredients, all of a sudden chicken and strawberry salads, tacos tartare, and trios of mini hamburgers are everywhere, and you find yourself craving simpler things like puréed soup, pasta with just salt and pepper, and shepherd's pie without all the fuss and extras — just meat and potatoes with a sprig of fresh rosemary on top.

And while I have not seen it all, I've seen *a lot*.

Edible menus are now a thing. And there are whole establishments dedicated to serving just cupcakes, noodles, or hot dogs. To me that makes about as much sense as those Japanese-English advertising slogans that you occasionally see on T-shirts or on Japanese sodas, like "Green Breeze Sound Sofa," "Brains Organic Form," "Jive Passion Talk," "I Feel Coke," and "The Fanky Tomato Stuff."

Gourmet hot dog and hamburger places now pepper big cities, and while it is nice to have a change from the two or three varieties from the last twenty or so years, it can be a little much. Some guy named Jeff Weinstein created the Counter restaurants, specializing in "Custom Built Burgers." The Counter offers "over 300,000 burger combinations."

I think this is what author of *The Paradox of Choice: Why More Is Less* was getting at. Sometimes more is not better.

Mini hamburgers became a popular appetizer for a time. They are often called "sliders," and can be had at a lot of weddings and functions. Some restaurants still have them on the menu, but this too shall pass despite their Kobe beef or rare tuna contents, or a meatball version (which made the September 2007 cover of *bon appétit*). Best bet for a teeny burger? Those ones at White Castle look pretty mouth-watering.

People are always looking for the next big thing. Sometimes it is a single ingredient, like the recent incarnation of chefs using carrot greens (the gangly tops of carrots), and sometimes it is a whole concept, such as sustainable seafood or tapas.

Don't get me started on tapas. Tapas, or shared plates, is a craze that chefs love because they can create relatively simple yet flavorful fare and people are apt to order a bunch of things, which chefs are always striving for as well. For a while there, there was a new tapas joint creeping up every couple of weeks. And while it is fun and sexy to go into a small intimate place and order wine and little plates with friends or your husband, it is no way for a person to eat. For a couple of months, I covered a number of tapas joints and I was constantly hungry. Olives do not a meal make — even if they're stuffed with anchovies, almonds, and salmon.

Coffee places like Tim Hortons and Starbucks, where it used to be all about coffee and something to eat on the way to the office, have become whole restaurants where you can now have sandwiches, fresh fruit snacks, and other tempting offerings of food stuff.

Pan-Asian fast-food restaurants have taken over the planet. You can now get pad thai, spring rolls, beef with broccoli, sushi, kimchee, and noodle soup on practically every major city corner. This is also spreading to other markets — Mediterranean, Mexican, and Middle Eastern to name the big ones. The good thing about these trends is they offer healthier fast food than the usual burger and pizza joints that were our go-to places as we were growing up. So now even at family restaurants, you can often get a Greek salad, ceviches, and perhaps even a falafel plate.

Now quality thin-crust pizzas with exciting and exotic toppings can be had at a number of joints outside of pizza parlors. I love a good thin, crisp crust, and some restaurants have done an excellent job. The simpler, the better in my books, but I've had some lovely tandoori chicken, seafood, and Peking duck versions. I have just one word of advice — skip the dessert pizza. They are never as good as you hope they'll be. In fact, they'll be much, much worse.

One way to not go hungry is to head out to one of the new steakhouses that are taking the country by storm. Sure there are vegetarian, vegan, and organic movements, but steak continues to be a top draw for going out for dinner. But go to the ATM first. You're going to need it — these places aren't cheap, despite the large size of the meat and sides.

People have also been increasingly influenced by celebrity chefs. They see Jamie, Mario, and Rachel cook meals on television, and want to have the same thing both at home and when they go out to eat. Trouble is, what you don't see are the food stylists, the people doing the grocery shopping and filling the fridge. See those little bowls filled with julienned carrots, scallions, and meat? That just saved the host an hour or two of work, and made it look like you too could cook a whole roast capon, and make your own pasta in twenty-two or forty-three minutes.

And local fare is getting a real push on menus — now you can eat local, seasonal food prepared by an expert (sometimes referred to as "haute barnyard"). The best of all worlds in the eyes of most foodies. And while I agree that it is delicious and great for the community and farmers and such, if you eat out as much as I do, it can get tiring having butternut-squash soup, ravioli filled with wild mushrooms and leeks, salad greens upon salad greens (or should I say mesclun greens upon arugula salad), or roasted beet salad night after night. How can that be, you ask, when everyone's preparing it so differently? While most chefs have a signature way of preparing their food, local fare is often largely untouched compared to regular menu items so the accoutrements, shall we say, are far less with farm-fresh squash and tomatoes. Which means, you are eating a lot of lightly seasoned food that is available for only a limited amount of time. I'm not against it by any means, but by my third roasted squash side, I'm ready for the seasons to change.

One month pork belly was so en vogue that every fine dining restaurant had it. Sure it was organic and incredibly fresh, but do you *know* what pork belly is? It's the part of the pig where bacon comes from, but is largely fat, with an incredibly hard seared outer edge. Picture it, hot fat in a two-inch by two-inch square. On its own. Just there for you to enjoy and savor.

Except that it's a two-by-two square inch of pork fat.

Am I ever glad *that* trend passed! Though I do still see it on menus from time to time, I avoid it like sponge toffee, fur, the Rubik's Cube comeback, and alleys behind butcher shops.

Homemade desserts have become not only commonplace, but a must for any restaurant that wants to be taken seriously. Thank goodness. Though I could really do without the crème brûlée of the month and molten chocolate cakes. Bite-sized versions are hot, and exotic ice creams and sorbets are exciting the crowds lately. And yes, sometimes they're a nice change of pace, but don't get too crazy with them, chef. I don't want quail egg and beer sorbet, got that? And any dessert over ten dollars is asking for trouble.

For those of you dessert lovers out there — be warned! Those sumptuous desserts that sound so good with dried plums? Those would be prunes, my friend. And remember when your dessert (pie, cake, or ice cream) was listed at the bottom of the page along with the prices of coffee and tea? Ahh. Such simpler times. Now you get a whole other menu, or sometimes even a whole new book that sighs as it hits the table.

Oh. Have you heard this one? We're requesting smaller portions now? It seems that diners are tiring of the gigantic servings and are asking restaurateurs to cut back in the name of worries about obesity and overeating. It's hard to believe, I know, but I've actually heard it straight from the mouths of chefs as well. I think it's a small group wanting less to eat and they're certainly not the majority. So I say bring on the big portions — if we wanted to eat sensibly, we'd eat at home.

You can now eat at "Fast Casual" and "Casual Fine Dining" restaurants. What does this mean exactly? Well, you eat good food fast in a nicer setting than an Arby's or the like, and it's less expensive than you'd be charged in a fine-dining establishment. This trend is on the rise. People want good food fast all the time, but they don't necessarily want to be downing sandwiches in their car, or sitting in a fast-food restaurant with sticky tables. And they want healthy, fresh food that is also reasonably priced. It's a hard balance to achieve, but the few places that do it well do it really well, and can earn a legion of lifelong fans.

There's a place like this in our 'hood that we go to a lot. They have whole-wheat pizzas, homemade pastas with creamy sauces, and organic ground beef, chicken, and vegetables, not to mention tantalizing salads like the mango, avocado, and curry I tend to favor. The food comes out quickly and you can eat really well for not much more than getting soup and a sandwich at Subway or the like. It's a trend that I see both when I'm out reviewing restaurants and also with my friends. Life has become so busy that healthy food on the go is a priority for most of us, but we also want to be pampered, if just a little. Sitting down for forty-five minutes or an hour and eating well is a compromise we're willing to make. We just need to find the places that are doing it and doing it right.

until the day i die

"Writing is simply a way of life before all other ways, a way to observe the world and to move through life, among human beings, and to record it all above all and to shape it, to give it sense, and to express something of myself in it."

— William Goyen

PEOPLE OFTEN ASK me what prompted me to become a writer. After thinking about it a lot, I think it comes down to a number of factors.

One is being born and raised in Toronto. Having lived here all of my life, I have been privy to the extreme advantages of living in a big and always bustling city.

Having parents who fostered my interests and who were artists themselves helped. I took (free) dance, art, animation, music, magic, calligraphy, and cooking classes. My dad and I walked along Queen West every Saturday morning (something we continue to do). I took the subway to each end of the city and discovered my love of the neighborhoods — Bloor West Village, the Annex, Queen West, Chinatown, Greektown, etc. My mom and I walked once a week to the Beaches, to Yonge and Lawrence, or anywhere our feet took us. It didn't matter. We were not only connecting, but discovering things about the city, and thus, ourselves.

I grew up reading too. My parents not only read, but considered it a way of learning, so that is why I read. This might be why I am drawn to nonfiction in such a fierce manner. I also read as a teenager as a way of improving myself. I felt stuck as a teen, like I wasn't going anywhere. I wasn't sure what I wanted to do "when I grew up," while friends were already getting solidified in bank jobs and going to university. Reading was a way to learn constantly. I read everything there was about the Algonquin Round Table, and came to love Dorothy Parker. I read about writing and writers, without knowing that this is how I would spend the rest of my days. I read to quench my need to learn, to be mentally stimulated and wowed on a constant basis.

I have always written letters. I write to people who never write back and sometimes have lovely correspondences with friends, but I always loved to write letters. My mom and dad write letters too, though it developed organically, not as something we ever spoke about or were taught.

One day back in 1997, I was reading the umpteenth book review and thought, hell, I read ten books a month (I only do about five or six now) — I could do this. So I queried a small, free writing newspaper, and I reviewed for them for three years.

I continue to write book reviews, but it is the essays, articles, and columns that thrill me. To write about a person, place, event, or thing — and know that I have nailed the description, or have someone say that they felt like they were there — to me, there is nothing better.

I write in a conversational style. The books always say, "Write how you talk," and that's what I strive to do. I want people to feel like I am whispering in their ear, can you believe this happened, wait until you see this place for yourself. I want to inspire people.

I admire several writers and their writing styles, which have been big influences on me. Susan Orlean's book *The Bullfighter Checks Her Makeup: My Encounters with Extraordinary People* has been a big influence on the way I write. She interviewed a variety of people and managed to tell their stories in completely different ways throughout the book. Do you realize how hard that is? This woman is talented. I also admire the style of Chuck Klosterman, a rock writer for *SPIN* magazine (I love his books too). He is smart and funny, which I think is extremely difficult to pull off. And he writes unabashedly about loving bad music, something that I am eternally grateful for, for I love Def Leppard, Boston, and Asia in ways that I cannot explain. Then there's Steve Martin's writing, which is melancholy, smart, moving, and ever so graceful, especially in his novel *Shopgirl*. His skill in drawing out moments and allowing for long silences is impeccable.

I think most of all I try to drink everything in. My curiosity is insatiable and can actually keep me up at night. I can focus on the big picture, but it is usually the details that are of interest. The way her hand went to her pendant necklace when she started talking about her boyfriend, the smell of the vindaloo, incense, and the waiter's cologne at Little India.

Writing is what I want to spend the rest of my life doing.

Being a writer is a lot like being a chef — each day you get up and try to create something new while maintaining the stuff that you have to crank out every day. They are careers that you only pursue because it is something that is inside you — otherwise you would not be able to handle all of the hardships and adversities that come with it. Both sound like dream jobs when you see the final result — the book or the byline, the stuffed chicken breast or the towering dessert. But what you don't see are the mistakes along the way, the long days and nights, and hands covered in flour and jam.

They are both incredibly rewarding at sporadic moments — when a customer raves about your duck, or when someone tells you how moved they are by a passage that you wrote. But mostly, we keep our heads down and do the work each and every day, trying to improve, trying to create something wondrous.

There are a lot of perils to writing. I haven't made much money at it, and while I've been working away at it for a decade, I still have little to show for it. But I write because I don't want to do anything else but this.

I don't know how it's going to work out financially, but I just have to trust that I can do it. I have faith in myself. That's what gets me up every day.

That and wondering what Brad and Angelina are up to.

Closed. Will reopen at 6 A.M.

outro and shout-out to my peeps

To all the **people attempting the writing life** — may your pen flow freely and your deadlines get extended.

To all of the **people who have supported me** in my life, both past and present — thanks for believing in me.

The **music** that started it all — for as long as I can remember I have had to get up outta my chair to dance to the beat. You are *never* too old to sing into the mirror with a brush as a microphone.

The **books and magazines** that I read along the way.

The **editors of magazines, websites, and newspapers** who encouraged and published my scrawling. Forever in your debt.

The **Toronto Public Library System** that has fostered me through my childhood, teens, and adulthood, bringing me the ultimate comfort of books, magazines, and CDs. The **Staff** for their help — thank you for allowing me fifty holds at a time, which turns out to be just enough to keep me engaged. Though is there any way I could get that extended?

My **sweet little laptops** that have been with me throughout it all, and for lasting as long as they did.

To my **Palm Treo** and **HTC TyTN**. I got more writing done on these little suckers than you'd ever believe. They are my favorite gadgets, my go-to tools, and, in the case of a pretty quick book deadline, my lifesavers.

To everyone who's supported **The Knack**, and for all those lovely folks who've sent me stuff to write about, I couldn't have done it without you. And my readers.

ECW Press for publishing a book by me, **and especially Jen Hale**, my editor who believed that I could write a good, funny book. And then helped form it into just that. My hearty thanks to everyone at ECW who helped get this onto the bookshelves — copyeditor Emily Schultz, cover designer David Gee, designer and typesetter Melissa Kaita, and publicists Simon Ware and Sarah Dunn.

To all **the chefs, restaurant owners, managers, and staff** who kept me in elasticized waistbands these last years.

And **those who made the biggest difference**:

My family: Mom (Ruth Cameron), Dad (Larry Dickison), Dogs and Brothers-In-Arms (Rip and Bogie) — your unconditional love and support has never wavered, not even during my teen years. Right back atcha. And to **Scott's family**: Henry and Bernice Albert, Grandma Albert, Paula and Jordan McNaught, and Grandma Pauline for accepting me into your family as if I was your own.

The love of my life Scott Albert. You make everything better and brighter each and every day. All of my love.

And **Cosmo**. I am so grateful to have you in my life. Thank you for always jumping on my lap, snuggling up to me at bedtime and in the morning, and for sitting on my work.

My peeps at 849. You are my neighbors, but more importantly, my friends and family. And you dropped by, giving me much-needed breaks from writing. Thank you Darren Berberick and Ben Walsh, Ryan Duggin and Sarah Doherty, Allana Gowan, Vawn Himmelsbach, Jeffrey Lerman and Jonah Crespo, and Paul A. Teolis.

My friends — Carol Barbour, Camille Djokoto, Chris Garbutt,

Ava and Rick Green, Heather Greenwood-Davis, Quyen Ha, Victoria Kerber, Wayne Lam, Jennifer LoveGrove, Alan McCullough and Teresa Martin, John McFetridge and Laurie Reid and the boyz, Kristen Manieri, Teresa Montanino, Norm Perry, Allison Plamondon and Eddie Glen, Penny Plautz, a great editor whom I have never met — Jeff Reich, Shelley Savor, Dan Wagstaff, and Cindy Woo.

And to **those who helped along the way, even if they don't know it** — Jully Black, Beverly Bowen, Eric Broers, Susan Brown, Degan Davis, Ellen DeGeneres for always being authentic and showing the world you just gotta get up and dance, Joan Didion, Cory Doctorow, Elizabeth Downes, Lionel Felix, Taliaferro Jones, Jack Foster, Marta Green, Christopher Guest, Chuck Klosterman for making people sit up and take notice of pop culture and rock writing, Amy Krouse Rosenthal for one of the best books ever, Bernie Mac, my hero Steve Martin, Marilyn, Katey Morley's EP *Phor* that started it all and that I listened to more than any other, Susan Orlean, Dorothy Parker, PFY and all the folks who worked there, Sylvia Plath, Stratos Papachristopoulos and Telly Damoulianos at Dine.TO, Yvonne Rose, Jerry Seinfeld, Jon Stewart, Tweety, Sharron Wall, and Maureen Williamson.

Journalist, essayist, and cultural critic Stephanie Dickison has contributed to several non-fiction books and encyclopedias and has written hundreds of articles for national and international magazines and newspapers. Her feature writing has appeared in the *Toronto Star, Washington Asia Press, The Writer, Pan,* PCWorld.ca, MacWorldCanada.ca, and dozens of other publications. She lives in Toronto. Her website is at www.stephaniedickison.com.